Never Too Far

THOMAS CHRISTOPHER

Kalmaha Press

Cover Design by Kalen O'Donnell

ISBN: 0615813658
ISBN-13: 978-0615813653

2nd Edition

For Jessica, Holton, and Vance

PART ONE

COUNTRY

Chapter 1

Joe slung the rifle strap over his shoulder and pointed, but his older brother Frank didn't say anything.

"Don't you see it?" Joe said. "Right there. Across the river."

Frank stepped back suddenly.

"We need to get out of here," Frank said. "Someone might still be there." He looked across the river again.

"What's it doing out here?"

"It looks abandoned," Joe said.

"That doesn't mean anything."

"We got to check it out."

Joe moved forward but Frank grabbed his arm.

"No we don't," Frank said. "Besides, you can't go walking up to it like any old piece of junk. It isn't something you leave lying around, either. They're coming back for it, for sure."

"All the more reason why we should go see it."

"That's not what I'm saying. I'm saying we shouldn't mess with it."

"Well, I'm going," Joe said.

At the river's edge, Frank snatched the rifle from Joe.

"I'm leading the way," Frank said.

Joe was about to grab the rifle back when Frank jammed the last shell into the open breech. He used his maimed hand, the one missing three fingers, and locked the bolt in place. Joe figured there was no sense in arguing now.

After they waded across the shallow river, they crouched low and crept up the rocky embankment to the old road. Frank raised his head to take a look, and then Joe poked his head up too.

"I don't think this is a good idea," Frank said. "It's definitely an Arbyter."

Joe couldn't take his eyes off it. He had never seen a real Arbyter before. What he knew about them came from Frank when he was in the city of Chikowa over a year ago. He said he saw Arbyters patrolling the streets all the time. The way Frank described them made Joe think of a beast on wheels, one with two dark windows in front like menacing eyes and a big machine gun on top like a horn.

"I'll go," Joe said.

"No, you won't," Frank said. "I'm going. Stay behind me."

For a moment Frank seemed afraid to go near the vehicle, which was flipped on its side. He stood with his legs spread and the rifle pointed at it as if he thought it might spring to life at any second. He shuffled forward. His wet shoes scraped on the dirt road. When he got close enough to touch the armored underbelly, he stopped. He nudged his foot against the scratched and dented metal. Then he stepped back, ready to fire, ready for it to finally awaken and show its true self. When it didn't move, he took his maimed hand off the rifle and motioned toward Joe.

"Come on," he whispered. "Stay behind me."

Joe jumped to his feet and hurried to his older brother who was rounding one of the Arbyter's huge front tires. Joe couldn't resist brushing his fingers along the tire's thick tread or touching the fang-like spokes in the grill on his way past. But the very second he turned the corner and saw the top of the Arbyter, he pulled up short. It was much stockier than what he imagined. It looked like the head of a giant iron bull. The dark eyes staring out from the squat cab were cracked and pitted from bullet fire, and the machine gun's long barrel was wedged tight in the ground.

Frank hung the rifle over his shoulder, climbed onto the machine gun, and heaved himself up onto the Arbyter's side. Once he got to his feet, he jabbed the rifle tip through an open window, or perhaps it was an open door. Joe didn't know because he couldn't see that high.

"Come up and look inside," Frank said. "I'll keep an eye out."

Joe scampered onto the machine gun and crawled up near Frank's feet. Painted on the Arbyter's door was the symbol of the Guardian Party, the ruling government in Chikowa. The symbol was a seven-pointed red star with a white ring in the middle and a red circle inside like a bull's eye.

"See if there're any dead soldiers in there," Frank said.

Joe got on his stomach and ducked his head inside the open window. He braced himself for a gory sight, but he didn't see any of the dead soldiers Frank was afraid of. Instead, he saw some kind of reddish-black substance splashed all around. He reckoned it was probably blood. He looked over the instrument panel, gazed at the cracks in the tinted windshield, and then craned his neck to look behind the seats. Nothing was there as far as he could tell.

On his way out, he gripped the steering wheel and even jiggled it once before he let go.

After he sat up, he said, "No bodies, but there's blood."

"They must've evacuated already."

"What do you think happened? Do you think it was attacked?"

"If it was, we wouldn't be standing here." Frank looked around like he was expecting someone to be there. "Let's get down."

Frank shouldered the rifle and shimmied down onto the machine gun. Joe began to follow him but then he thought of something.

"Hey," he said. "I bet it still has fuel."

Joe scooted to the back end of the Arbyter to look for the fuel plate. As soon as he found it, he pried it open, unscrewed the cap, and stuck his nose into the open cylinder. He took a big whiff. The smell of the fumes made his eyes water. It still had fuel. He couldn't believe it. He stared at Frank standing on the ground below.

"Get down from there," Frank said.

"How much do you think it's worth?"

"How should I know? I don't even know how much is in there."

Joe was going to find out. He looked into the woods and spotted a big fallen limb. He leapt off the Arbyter, forgetting how high up he was, and stumbled hard to his knees. But the drop barely fazed him. He ran to the fallen limb, planted his foot on it, and snapped off a long thin branch.

"What are you doing?" Frank said. "Are you crazy?"

Back at the Arbyter, Joe clambered up to the fuel tank. He dipped the stick into the opening and fed it down the pipe as far as it would go. The smell rushed up into his nose again. He pulled the stick out to find it half-soaked with diesel.

"There's like half a tank."

"Let me see that," Frank said.

Joe handed the stick down to Frank.

"You know how much this is worth?" Frank said.

"I already asked you that."

"It was at ten thousand shekels when I was in Chikowa."

"So you were lying."

"So what? That might not even be right."

"You think that's close, though?"

"It's got to be. This is like gold."

"Why don't we sell it?"

"Don't be nuts. We get caught with this, we'll be executed. It's illegal to have. You know that. Forget about it." Frank threw the stick into the woods. "Put that cap back on and get down from there."

"I'm serious," Joe said.

"Get it out of your head because it's not happening."

"I could do it."

"What did I just say? No way."

"But you went."

"And look what happened to me." He shoved his maimed hand up at Joe. "You aren't going. I'm not going. Nobody's going. Got it?"

Once they crossed the river, they walked through the wooded bluffs and down into the valley where Joe's family farm stood. Even though it didn't look much different from any other farm Joe had seen, he knew it was a ramshackle wreck. The stark buildings were aged and weathered. The splitting wood was streaked gray and black. Off to the side of the barn was a rickety fence that held the little livestock they had left—a wooly goat, two spotted hogs, some chickens, and the horses, Lester and Sam. Beyond that was a field of limp corn and a garden of scraggly vegetables. The house leaned to one side as if it was constantly trying to hang on against a fierce wind. Broken windows were covered in plastic or scraps of wood. It was a wonder anyone lived there.

Chapter 2

Joe's family was gathered around the kitchen table, except for Mom. She was lying in bed recovering from one of her episodes where her mind got all jumbled. The room was hot and the air musty. Despite the open window above the sink and the open back door, there was no breeze to speak of. The heat stayed trapped and settled its heavy weight in the kitchen.

The silence was nearly unbearable. Joe shoved his fingers through the front of his hair. Sweaty strands stood up like pieces of straw.

"And you didn't see anyone else there?" Dad finally said.

"We searched all over," Frank said. "We didn't see a thing."

Dad raked his fingers through his gray beard. A fly glided past his shoulder and landed on the table.

Joe could hardly stand it anymore. Why was Frank taking so long to reveal the most important thing?

"It's got half a tank of diesel in it," Joe blurted.

Frank shot Joe a scornful look, but Joe didn't care.

"We got to get it before someone else does," Joe said. "It's worth a fortune according to Frank."

"Leave me out of this," Frank said.

"We got more mouths to feed. You said it yourself, Dad."

Joe looked at the pregnant orphan girl. The top of her swollen belly peeked above the table like a loaf of bread. She lowered her head to the point where her chin pressed tight against her collarbone. Her long yellow hair hung around her face like a shroud. Mom said her baby could come at any time now. The girl was only fourteen, two years younger than Joe. She never spoke as far as he knew. Sometimes you didn't even know she was there, and you were surprised to see her suddenly even though she'd been there the whole time.

"You said the money Frank got from the city won't last," Joe continued. "All we got is this burnt up land that doesn't have much more to give. That's what you said. That diesel could be our salvation."

"It's a crime," Dad said. "If they find it on us, it's a death sentence. No questions asked." He combed his beard. "Besides, it's against the *Word of Virid*."

"Come on," Joe said. "We would be stupid not to. Where else could we get that kind of money?"

Dad shook his head. "Forget about it. It's wrong. Just leave it. And pretend we never knew about it."

"But—"

"You heard him," Frank interrupted.

"But what's going to happen to us without more money? Don't you see what I'm saying?"

"Virid will provide," Dad said. "We'll have enough to feed ourselves."

"For how long? What happens when the last of our livestock is gone? When Lester and Sam are gone? Then what? What about the orphan girl and her baby? What about Mom and her mind getting more and more scrambled?"

"And money is going to solve that?" Dad said. "What does money buy us out here, anyway? There is nothing to buy. Don't you get that? There is hardly anything left. It's dried up. The town's dried up. The ground's dried up. The wind picks it up and carries it away. It's gone, and it isn't coming back, ever." He stopped and scratched at his beard, digging and clawing into the bushy thicket. "There's no point," he said.

"So you want to just give up," Joe said.

"That's enough!" Frank said.

Joe stormed out of the kitchen and went to the barn. He left the doors open and a long shaft of light sunk deep into the interior. It coated the rusty steel on the pickup wagon and brightened the strips of yellow straw stamped into the barn's dirt floor. Dust floated in the air, which smelled of manure and rot. Joe plopped down on an overturned bucket beside the gate to the horses' pen.

This was his chance to help his family, Joe thought. This was his time, just like Frank had helped when he went to Chikowa to work in the steel mill. If Joe could figure out a way to sell that diesel, he could change his family's future. They wouldn't have to give up like all the rest. They wouldn't have to admit defeat and live as dregs in the city's slums, where their lives would be no better than rats, according to Frank, where they'd have to work backbreaking jobs every day just to feed themselves, where they'd be under threat of abuse or imprisonment at any time, where poor dregs like them would have to sell their organs or limbs or unborn babies just to survive. Is that what Frank wanted? Is that what his family wanted? To slowly shrivel up out here and then crawl into the city and waste away there?

Besides, Dad didn't know what he was talking about when he said money couldn't buy anything out here. That wasn't the point. He was just getting bitter. Although it was dangerous, they could travel north again and buy wooly goats and spotted hogs from the Hickaba tribes. They could even go to the city for that matter and get supplies there. The money would give them options. That was the point. And Joe didn't care about disobeying the Word of Virid. He didn't care if he was stealing. Maybe that diesel was a gift from Virid, and it would be wrong to refuse it.

After a while, Frank appeared at the barn door. His figure looked like a shadow against the bright column of light streaming in.

"I can do it," Joe said.

"It's not happening. Get it through your thick head."

"You went."

"I went there to work. And you'd be going there to sell diesel on the black market. Something that will get you killed if you get caught. That's a big difference."

"I don't care what you say."

"How are you going to do it, then?"

"I don't know."

"It's not worth it, Joe. It's not worth the risk. We'll make it."

"Be honest. You really think we'll make it, especially with the orphan girl and her baby? Be honest."

Frank didn't say anything.

"See."

"See, nothing. Face the facts. It's like Dad said. You've seen the size of the dusters that have been blowing through here now. We're not dirt-eaters for nothing. This is going to be dead land. Whether we get rich off that diesel or not, you can't live off dead land."

"You know where we'll end up."

"And that's worth your life?"

"I won't get caught."

"Don't count on it."

"So you're saying we're supposed to wait until we're skin and bones and have to drag ourselves into the city just to survive?"

"At least we'll all be together."

"I don't believe you."

"It's the truth."

"You said you would never go back there."

"If it's the only choice we have, I'll go," Frank said.

"But it's not the only choice. Let me take the diesel."

"No."

"I'll do it anyway. You and Dad can't stop me."

"Don't be an idiot."

"I'm doing it. It's my turn."

"Your turn? This isn't a game. You don't have any idea what's out there."

"Try and stop me."

Frank shook his head. "How? You can't just walk in there with it. There are guards and police everywhere. Chances are you wouldn't even make it that far. And even if you did, you're only a worthless dirt-eater. They'll do you like they did me."

"I can do it."

"Listen to me. You want to know what happens to you out there? You get massacred. Sometimes for no reason. In the forest I saw busted-up trailer wagons and pickup wagons strewn along the side of the road with the dead bodies of morons just like you. They weren't just dead either. They were chopped up and scattered on the road. Severed arms, legs, heads, hacked-up bodies. Guts spilled out. That's what it means out there."

Chapter 3

Frank led the way through the dark woods. The alcohol lantern swayed from the only finger on his maimed hand. The light cast a yellow glow that brushed against the tree trunks and splashed on the ground. It made the darkness seem blacker beyond the lantern's shaking light. A possum's pink eyes gleamed like something alien before it scuttled away. Joe clutched the five-gallon bucket with the rubber hose inside.

"Did you talk to the girl?" Frank said.

"I talked to her. She nodded her head like she understood. But I don't know if she did or not."

"This is crazy," Frank said.

The day before, Joe finally got Frank to consent to his plan of taking the diesel into the city. During the night a small duster had blown through and showered everything with a layer of gritty dust. They'd been in the vegetable garden brushing the dust off the meager plants. Frank carefully cleaned off all the limp leaves with a damp rag and picked off the dead withered ones, while Joe hurried from plant to plant and from row to row. It wasn't like it mattered anymore. He no longer felt his family's life depended on the survival of these barely living plants. The diesel would be their savior. He knew it. He felt it. He had to convince Frank.

"That just goes to show how dumb you are," Frank said. "The black market isn't a real place."

"What is it, then?"

"It's a secret."

"Then how do you know?"

"Everybody knows. It's not that kind of secret. It's a secret because it's a crime."

"Think of the money. Think of it. We could buy enough food to keep us here even if everything does dry up and go dead. Maybe we could go northwest to the 'promised lands' like other people. You know what they say. Water flows from the mountains and all kinds of food hangs from the trees for the taking."

"That's all a load of crap. How many times do I have to tell you not to believe that stuff? There is only one paradise—Welkenglebe, the home of Virid—and all the rest are lies."

"That money will give us a chance, and you know it."

"It will also get you killed. These black market people aren't like regular peddlers, Joe. These are dangerous men."

"Either help me, or I'm doing this alone," Joe said. "I've made up my mind."

"Don't be a fool."

"You're a fool for not wanting to do anything to save us. Do you want to live like cowards? Do you want to be a coward?"

Frank slapped Joe across the face. Joe's head snapped to the side. His cheek stung. What he'd said about Frank wasn't fair, and he knew it. He deserved the slap. But he was so frustrated that nobody wanted to do anything about their family's survival (when a huge chance had landed right in their lap!) that he'd said something he didn't mean.

"I don't want to hear another word," Frank said.

"I'll find a way. It'll be harder without you, but I'll find a way. I'm doing it. With or without you."

"I'm telling you, you won't make it."

"The blood will be on your hands."

Frank didn't say anything. He spit on the ground and then rubbed it with the heel of his shoe before he walked away.

At the edge of the river, which shone silver in the moonlight, Frank put out the alcohol lantern. They would make the rest of their way by moonlight. Before they crossed, Frank wanted to check the transistor. He'd made a deal with Joe. He told him if they heard anyone looking for the Arbyter, they would turn back and go home. Frank twisted the dial, but all they heard were crackles and fuzz. That was all they ever heard.

"The coast is clear," Joe said. "I told you. Nobody's looking for it."

"Doesn't make any sense."

"It doesn't have to make any sense. Come on."

"Okay, okay, settle down."

They stepped into the river's sluggish current. The sound of the water seemed amplified in the dark stillness and seemed to echo as if in a canyon. They waded slowly along until they got to a sandbar where they rested a minute. Joe looked up river. The dark water snaked through the bluffs and into the night sky as if it were flowing into the stars.

When they reached the embankment, they crawled up to the road. Frank slowly approached the wrecked Arbyter like he still didn't trust it. They walked around to the other side and then climbed up on top. Frank fished a small box of matches out of his shirt pocket. He struck one against the base of the lantern and lit the mantle. Light quivered against the Arbyter's metal and against the symbol of the seven-pointed red star with the bull's-eye in the middle. Joe flipped open the fuel plate and unscrewed the cap. He shoved one end of the hose down into the tank.

"Let me get it started," Frank said.

He wrapped his mouth around the hose and sucked, but he must not have pulled away quick enough because he made an awful gagging sound.

"Frank?" Joe said. "You okay?"

Frank turned his head and hacked, but in the process he knocked the lantern off and it hit the ground and rolled away. Joe grabbed the tip of the hose, bubbling with diesel, and jammed it into the five-gallon bucket. He looked at Frank again, who was on his hands and knees now, coughing and retching.

"Frank?" Joe said.

He scooted beside his brother as Frank rammed a finger down his throat. His body convulsed. He choked and retched again until a gush of vomit spewed out. Some of it splashed on Joe's pants, but he didn't care. He touched his brother's hunched back. It trembled. Frank turned to sit upright again and plunked right down in his own puke. His eyes watered, wetting his cheeks. Drool hung from his lips.

"Frank," Joe said, "say something."

"I'm okay," Frank said, his voice hoarse. "Check the diesel."

"There's only a little bit coming out now," Joe said.

He looked closer and examined the liquid inside. It was about half full.

"Put the lid on," Frank said, "and let's get out of here."

Once they climbed down, Frank found the cracked lantern. Then they scurried down the rough embankment to the river. Frank stopped and slurped up a mouthful of water, swished it around in his mouth, and spit it out.

On the other side of the river, they hurried over the bluff and through the woods until they hit the flat valley. Joe looked up at the soaring night sky. For a few seconds he stared at the bright stars swooping and shining above their farm. He loved to do that. Gazing at the stars was one of his favorite things to do, but there was no time for any of that now.

Chapter 4

At the farm, Joe lugged the bucket of diesel inside the barn, where they poured it into a smaller red container. Frank located some deerskins and they wrapped them around the container and tied it up with twine to keep it secure. Frank said he wanted to make the bundle look like a bunch of skins that were being taken into the city to be sold. It wouldn't draw suspicion, especially with the story they came up with about why Joe and the pregnant orphan girl needed to go into the city in the first place.

Then they packed the wagon with supplies. Food and water, a foot trap, a bow and six arrows, blankets, firewood, a flint sparker, an extra knife, and a rusty fishing pole. Frank found the box of rifle shells hidden in a trap door near the back of the barn. He pulled it out and opened the rusty metal box. There were two leather pouches of bullets inside—one for the old bolt-action rifle and one for the Calvin lever-action rifle.

When Frank picked up the Calvin pouch, Joe was surprised, and a little excited.

"How many of them you need?" Frank said. There were only thirty shells left.

Joe thought for a moment. "All of them."

"You can't take all of them." Frank counted out ten. "Now that's all you get, so be smart with them. Don't go wasting them."

"I won't. Food and protection only."

"Protection only. If you get low on food, forage and trap. As a last resort, use the arrows."

Frank held out the shells in his good hand. The cuff on his green shirt rode up his wrist and revealed a thick purplish scar. It was from where he had scraped the city's identification number off his skin and from where he had cut down a quarter inch to make sure he dug out the translucent veritag. After Joe stuffed the shells in his pocket, Frank put out the lantern and they left the barn.

They walked over to the well to get a drink. Above the dark bluff along the river was a sweeping sky of stars.

Frank pumped the handle and Joe leaned his head into the stream of musty water dribbling from the spout.

"You remember who to go to?" Frank said.

"The fat man," Joe said. He wiped his wet mouth.

"Templeton. Remember that name. He saved me."

"I know."

"You sure you can do it?" Frank said.

"I can do it."

They switched places and Joe pumped as Frank drank. Frank rested his damaged hand on the top of the spout while he cupped his good hand and splashed water on his face.

"If you don't make it," Frank said, "I won't be able to live with myself."

Joe looked at his older brother. He stared into Frank's weary eyes before Frank laid his wet hand on Joe's head.

"Be careful," Frank said. "You hear me? Just be careful."

Joe still recalled his brother's face on the day he returned from the city. The instant Joe saw Frank's horse plodding toward him in the distance, he sprinted across the dry ground shouting Frank's name. Joe was breathless by the time he got to his brother, but Frank didn't even acknowledge him. He stared straight ahead, his face lifeless and cold.

"Get on home and quit blubbering," he'd said.

Joe was stunned and hurt. Only later, when he saw the missing fingers and the scars across Frank's back, did Joe understand. At the steel mill, Frank got his hand caught in a slag wagon, and if not for a fat man named Templeton, who tore Frank loose, he might've been dragged to his death. The scars on his back were from being a dirt-eater.

In the house, they took off their shoes and went quietly up the stairs to the bedroom they shared. The curtains were open and moonlight brightened the dark room. Once Joe got into bed, he had a hard time keeping his eyes shut. He felt a little jumpy, or maybe fidgety. He couldn't tell. Maybe he was a tiny bit scared. Or maybe it was only nervousness excitement. Whatever it was, he was ready to go. He couldn't wait to go. All he could think about was getting to Chikowa and getting that money and returning home a hero.

Chapter 5

The following night, just as they planned, Joe and the pregnant girl snuck away while Mom and Dad slept. Frank hitched up the horses to the pickup wagon and rechecked the bundled-up container of diesel. It was hidden in a metal compartment below the wagon cab's floorboards. They'd made the compartment a while ago to hide valuables when traveling.

The wagon itself was fashioned from an old pickup. The front end was shorn off and the engine gone to scrap a long time ago. All the windows in the cab were busted out and the doors torn off. Inside, there wasn't any steering wheel, or stick shift or radio, because they had all been ripped out too. They were useless now. All the dials—the speedometer, the fuel gauge—were stripped of needles and the numbers faded to smudges. The seat was made of wood planks. Lashed over the wagon bed was a bonnet, like the kind on an old prairie schooner, only the bonnet was made of plastic tarps.

After Joe and the orphan girl were in the cab and ready to go, Frank reached out and touched the cuff of Joe's pants. He let the rough fabric drift through his thumb and fingertip. Joe looked down into Frank's moonlit eyes. Frank's mouth opened like he wanted to say something, but then it closed up again and he slapped the side of the wagon.

"Get going, then," he said.

Chapter 6

By daybreak, they were riding through a gently rolling land. The short copper-colored grass rippled in the hot wind like animal hair. Inside the cab, Joe hunched forward and held the reins loosely in his hands. The wagon rolled and swayed along the dirt road. Up ahead there was the shimmer of a hill on the horizon.

He pushed up the brim of his straw hat and looked at the pregnant girl. She bounced in the seat next to him, her head slung low beneath her floppy-brimmed hat. Her straight yellow hair swung like clothes on a line. She wore the same dress with the blue flowers she had worn yesterday. She had only three—the one she came to the house in and the two that Mom had made for her since. Her big belly sticking out still looked funny to Joe, like she was hiding a big ball underneath her dress. He was expecting at any minute for her to pull it out, to laugh like it was a joke, and look like a normal girl again. Joe wondered what the pregnant girl was thinking or if she was thinking at all.

He kept an eye out for a place to stop and rest. He was tired from traveling all night and morning. That's when he first saw the caravan as a thin trail of dust rising in the distance. As it got closer, the dust turned into a cloud. A while later, the shapes of the caravan began to appear and grow more distinct. Joe didn't know what to expect or what kind of people they might be, so he grabbed the Calvin rifle off the floor and cradled it in his lap. When the caravan was maybe half a mile away, he swerved the wagon to the left to give the caravan enough room to pass by. He wanted to avoid any confrontation or any appearance of being unfriendly. But he got nervous and stopped the wagon. He kept his hand on the Calvin rifle. His mouth was dry and sticky like paste.

The caravan stopped all of a sudden. Dust whirled around it. There were two campers and two long trailers pulled by teams of horses and bisox, which were an old genetic cross between a bison and an ox. Four lone riders on horseback wore matching brown hats. Two of the riders talked with each other until one turned his horse around and came galloping toward them. Sam whinnied as if he was going to be spooked, but Lester nudged him with his head as if telling him to calm down.

"It's okay, boys," Joe said.

But if everything was okay, why was the man charging at them so fast? Did he want to cause trouble? Intimidate them? If so, it was working. When the brown-hatted man was almost on them, he pulled his big gray horse up close to the side of the cab.

Lester and Sam reared up and Joe tugged on the reins. The wagon creaked. The man's horse stomped its hooves and turned in a circle. In one hand the man held a rifle upright against his thigh.

"It's okay, boys," Joe said to Lester and Sam again.

Once the man's horse settled down, he peered in at Joe and the pregnant girl. His eyes caught the rifle in Joe's lap. He had a bristly red beard and light brown eyes beneath furry red eyebrows. He smiled with yellow teeth and smelled like rotten meat.

"Where you headed?" His voice was deep.

"Going to Chikowa," Joe said. "My girl is pregnant and she needs a hospital. She's breech." That was the story he and Frank had come up with.

The man ducked lower and spied a curious look at the girl.

"You're nothing but kids," the man said.

"Our parents died of poxebola. We're all we got."

"PB? I heard there was a run of it out here."

"It's run out for now."

"For now," the man said. "You need anything?"

"We're okay."

"You got a ways until you reach the forest. There's a good camping spot a mile out in a little shantytown of about a hundred scavengers. Nice people but keep a good eye on your stuff. Watch out for marauders along the main road. They're ruthless."

"We're going up through the north," Joe said, before he realized Frank told him not to tell anyone the true way they were going.

"It's a lot longer that way. You sure you don't need anything?"

"We got enough."

The man squinted off toward the west like he was trying to make something out. There was nothing there but a bleached sky and shimmering heat waves.

"The forest and city aren't any place for good people." He shook his head. "We're headed northwest. To the coast, the 'promised lands.' If we make it. Isn't no other choice." The man squinted at Joe. "What do you got in there?" He flicked his head toward the back of the wagon.

"Things we need," Joe said.

The man lowered the barrel of his rifle so it was even with Joe's head.

"Hate to do this to you, but it's a matter of survival. You understand?"

Joe didn't understand. Did the man mean to shoot him? Joe stared out at the caravan and the other three horsemen. Two of them set off galloping toward the wagon, kicking up more dust, until they pulled up beside the rifleman. Joe was afraid to move his head to see what was going on. But out of the corner of his eye he glanced at the pregnant girl. She gripped bunches of her dress in tight little fists and squeezed her feet together.

"We're not here to rob them blind," the rifleman said to the others. "Take a few things we need, but leave them enough so they can survive."

Joe heard the squeak of saddles, the sound of hooves, and then the men rummaging and banging around in the wagon right behind his head.

"A big sack of breadroot," one of them said. He had a high-pitched voice and Joe wondered if it was a girl, not a man.

Someone cracked open a lid on a plastic water bucket.

"Buckets of water," came the other voice.

"Grab the sack and take some water," the rifleman said.

The wagon wobbled as they jumped out. When they rode up beside the rifleman again, he said, "Looks good."

Then the two thieves dashed off toward the caravan. The smaller one, the girl perhaps, was carrying the sack of breadroot. It was the only sack of breadroot they brought, and now it was gone, not even a day into their journey. The other thief held one of the plastic buckets of water by the handle, which left only four.

"We got women and children we need to tend to," the rifleman said. "You understand?"

"No, I don't understand," Joe said. "I got a pregnant girl with a baby inside her."

"We're all in this together. It's not personal."

"It's personal to us. That's our stuff you stole."

"Don't get all high and mighty on me. We left you plenty. Be grateful."

After the man rode off, Joe was even more upset. He was upset with himself for allowing this to happen. It was his own fault for being too nervous and for acting like a kid. It made them an easy target. The man must've figured out fairly quickly that he could rob them with no trouble. Joe should've raised his rifle as soon as the man pulled up, or he should've never stopped the wagon. The loss of the breadroot was a big blow. Now they only had the deer jerky, a bag of pinole, and the crate of canned food.

Soon enough, the caravan started moving again. Dust clouded up behind it. Joe decided to stay put until they passed by. The campers were patched together haphazardly with different colored sheets of metal and wood. The wood leaves over the windows were propped open with rods. Women and children peeked out the openings at Joe and the girl. Tied behind the last trailer were two scrawny cows that were no doubt going to be butchered before journey's end. The dust from the caravan drifted into the cab and floated like a mist until

27

Joe shook the reins and Lester and Sam lurched forward. The dust slowly cleared away. The heat waves wriggling on the horizon blurred the bleached sky and the hills ahead.

Chapter 7

Before nightfall he found a place to camp. After he made a fire, he poured a jar of bean soup into a pot and put it on the fire. He scooped some into a cup for the girl, but when he handed it to her, she didn't move. He set it on the ground next to her in case she wanted to eat it later. Then he spread the blankets on the ground for a bed and he got the rifle so it would be close. Once he sat down, he unwrapped his recorder that he kept in a square of leather cloth. He made the recorder himself from a block of wood. It took him days. He chopped, whittled, carved, and smoothed the wood into the instrument in his hands. After he twisted the two parts together, he licked the tip of the mouthpiece. He placed his thumb and his fingers on the holes and blew softly. A few mournful notes came out.

Joe played a little bit of an old song he'd learned from a tattered songbook. He hoped to get some kind of reaction out of the girl, but she only turned her head slightly before she let it hang low again like she didn't care.

He played some more and then stopped. What was the point? He listened to the silence and the occasional snap from the red embers. He looked at the stars salted across the sky. He felt lonely and anxious, especially after what happened to them that day. Being robbed at gunpoint on the first day wasn't exactly reassuring. He wanted to say something about it. He wanted to talk it out and feel better again. That's what talking did for him. He liked to discuss things the way he always did with Frank. But if the person you were talking to wasn't going to respond, or the person acted like you weren't even there, what was the use?

He tried to take his mind off it, so he thought about one of the songs that the old hermit Hans had taught him before he died last winter.

> I'm gonna run, better not catch me;
> I'm gonna run, better not catch me.
> I'm going home, Lord, Lord, I'm going home.

When he stopped singing, there was only silence again, and he wished the pregnant girl would finally say something, anything, even a grunt. An animal howled far in the distance, faint and fleeting. Joe listened hard for it again, but no sound came. Even though he played a few more songs, the girl didn't act like she heard a thing. Maybe she was asleep.

Chapter 8

The next day they crested a hill and slowly descended into another valley. The brown grass flashed with streaks of crimson. In the distance was a smattering of trees that resembled small green smudges. Joe figured it must be the creek Frank said was a good place to stop. Joe glanced at the pregnant girl. She had her head down, bobbing and swaying with the bumps and jolts of the wagon.

When they reached the creek, Joe found a cluster of scrub trees around a bend and pulled the wagon in. After he hopped out of the cab, he rubbed his sore butt and shook out his buzzing legs. He unhitched Lester and Sam so they could drink and munch for a while. Then he walked to the edge of the creek, where the yellowish water was clear enough that he could see some fish, which surprised him. Frank hadn't said anything about that.

He dashed over to the pregnant girl. She still sat slumped in the cab.

"Hey, there's fish in there," he said.

He grabbed her knee, which felt like a hard knot in a thin rope, and shook her leg. He didn't mean anything by it. He was only excited and wanted to rouse her. That was all. But she clawed his hand away from her knee. She dug her sharp nails into his skin and darted to the other end of the cab. Joe was stunned for a second, but he shouldn't have been, especially after what had happened with Frank. He touched her one time and she spooked like a rabbit and ran to a corner of the living room and hid.

"I told you not to touch her," Dad had said.

"But I barely did," Frank said.

"What did you need to touch her for anyway?"

"She seemed lost."

When Frank and Joe had come inside the house that day, she was standing at the sink, washing the dishes. She didn't seem to notice they were there. She seemed lost in another world. Joe was still getting used to her being in the house. She seemed so odd and out-of-place. Ghostly. He wasn't sure how to treat her. To be honest, he was kind of scared about doing the wrong thing. It was like trying to carry around an egg on a spoon.

As Joe watched her, she circled a dirty rag around a plate. He thought maybe there was something wrong with her. She kept going over the same plate like she wasn't ever going to stop. Frank must've been thinking the same thing because he walked up behind her and tapped her lightly on the shoulder. As soon as he did it, she whirled on him like he was trying to grab her. Her hair slashed through the air and slapped Frank's arm. Then she vanished for a moment, as if she really were a ghost, until Joe saw her streaking through the doorway. She lay huddled in a corner of the living room for the rest of the day.

"I didn't mean to scare you," Joe said to her now. "I just wanted to tell you about the fish and how I'm going to catch some for dinner. How's that sound? You like fried fish?"

The girl remained hidden beneath her floppy hat, totally unresponsive. And now he wished he hadn't touched her.

There wasn't much he could do at that point, so he got the fishing pole out of the wagon, grabbed the can of earthworms, and walked to the creek. After he poked a worm on the hook, he lowered it into the yellowish water and held it there. Soon enough, a fish struck and he reeled it in with the rusty reel. He wrenched the hook out and scooped up the fish. But he nearly dropped it when he saw the pregnant girl standing in front of him.

The fish wiggled.

"I caught one," he said.

The pregnant girl stood motionless, her head down, her hat pulled low. He didn't care how she was standing, though. He was simply glad she was standing at all and not hiding in the cab where he thought she might stay for the rest of the night. He held the shiny fish up to her, hoping she might look. She lifted her head slightly. He saw the point of her chin and the under-curve of her pink lower lip. She shuffled forward, maybe a couple of inches, but she didn't raise her head anymore or move her arms, which hung like sticks at her sides.

"How about you keep an eye on this one while I catch some more?" Joe said.

He laid the fish in the grass and it flopped and gasped for air. It had a few red lesions on it but it didn't look too bad. Joe had seen worse.

"Don't let him get away now."

Joe stood up and went toward the creek. He poked another worm on the hook and dropped it in. When he glanced behind him to see if the pregnant girl had moved, he found her sitting on the ground. He stepped back to see what she was doing. What he saw amazed him. She sat with her thin bony legs spread out in a V around the fish while she gently stroked and petted it, as if she were trying to soothe and comfort the poor thing in its slow gasping death. He felt a tug on his line and spun his head back to the creek. He jerked on the pole and reeled in another fish that he brought to the girl.

"Watch this one, too," he said, and set it in the girl's outstretched hands.

Later on, she helped clean the fish. After he gutted them with his pocketknife and cut out the lesions, he handed the fish to the girl. She took them to the creek to wash. Joe did his best to act like nothing unusual was going on and they'd cleaned fish together countless times. However, his insides were all abuzz. He even smiled a few times without even realizing it. As they worked, the sun sat bleeding away on the horizon.

Joe fried the fish, heads and tails and all, in the cast iron skillet. He set it on a rusty grill in the fire. The fish sizzled and steamed until their skin blackened and cracked and their eyes crusted brown. Joe pulled them out by their stiff tails and placed them on two tin plates. After Joe said a prayer, the pregnant girl tore at her fish. She ripped back the skin and sank her teeth into the white meat. Joe was hungry, too, but not that hungry. He was surprised at how ravenous she was, especially since she seemed so shy when they ate at home. You didn't even know she'd eaten until you noticed her plate was clean.

When they finished, Joe got out the bag of pinole. It was a mixture of ground corn, dried and ground tepary beans, crushed squash seeds, and sage. He barely got the bag open before the pregnant girl snatched it out of his hands. Apparently she wanted to make the cakes. She pulled a handful of pinole from the bag and poured some water on it from her cup. She mashed the mixture into a ball, padded it flat, and then slapped it in the skillet. Joe looked at her and smiled.

Afterwards, they washed the dishes in the creek and then got ready for bed. Stars started to pop and glow in the blue-black sky.

"You want a blanket?" Joe said.

The pregnant girl didn't respond. Which was okay. He was getting used to her silence. He felt more comfortable just talking, even if it felt like he was talking to himself. Maybe she was silent because of what happened to her before she came to live with them. He'd never really thought much about where she came from. It didn't seem that important. Besides, the girl was more of Mom's concern. He and Frank were supposed to steer clear of her. That was all changed now. Suddenly, knowing more about her seemed necessary. It seemed vital almost. The only problem with getting to know her was that she didn't talk.

He only knew that traders passing through the decrepit little village of Gunther had dumped her off at the temple with no explanation. Mom couldn't fathom not taking in this lost little lamb with child. Joe remembered Frank saying it was a bad idea to take her, but Dad said they could handle it and they couldn't turn their back on such a child in need. Mom fawned over her like she was her blood daughter. And for a while Mom's spirits seemed to rise.

Joe remembered when he first saw the pregnant girl. Her long stringy hair hung from a bone-white part in the center of her scalp. It hung in front of her drooping head like a separated curtain that someone was peering out of to see who was coming up the road. Even though she was rail thin in her dingy brown dress, he couldn't stop staring at her distended belly. She held the string handles of two boxes, which contained all her meager belongings. She was a sight to see, for sure.

Joe pulled his recorder out, fitted it together, and licked the tip.

"Anything you want to hear?" he said to the girl, not expecting her to answer. He just wanted to hear some human words, even if they were his own.

But then the girl spoke. She said, "Blackbird."

Joe sat up, startled, and stared at the girl. He was unsure if he really did hear her talk or if it was his imagination playing tricks on him.

"Blackbird?" he said. "Did you say 'Blackbird'?"

"Blackbird," she said again.

He was flabbergasted.

"You want to hear that?" he said. That was one of the songs from his tattered songbook. She must've recognized it from when he played it at home. "I know bunches of those songs from that book. Every one. Even the ones where the pages are missing and I only know half the song. I learned them all. Is that the one you want to hear? You like that one?"

Joe knew he was blathering on, but he was so shocked and delighted to hear the girl talk to him that words just tumbled out. He ended up playing the song twice, although the girl didn't act like she was listening. It didn't matter to Joe. He was simply happy that she'd responded to him. Even though it was only one word, it was better than nothing. He wanted to try to engage her in more conversation, to tease out some more words, but he thought he'd better not press his luck. *Blackbird*, he said to himself.

Chapter 9

The next day was grueling. The wagon cab felt like a furnace inside and Joe felt as if he were roasting in his own skin. Still, it was better than being exposed to the blistering sun, which would've cooked them even worse. Sweat soaked through his clothes and dripped off his nose. He thought the pregnant girl must've been burning up, too. He was afraid her baby might cook inside her like in an oven.

The land they traveled through was mostly burnt. Only a few stands of living trees slowly withered under the relentless burn of the heat. They traveled southward into the dry dusty lowlands and swung east where the land was burnt the color of faded blood and rocks were scorched white as wood ash.

The land hadn't always been this way. Everything changed after the temperature began to rise. The fertile prairies turned into arid plains, while the plains turned to dust, all the way west to the Milapske Mountains. The plainspeople, as they were called back then, left their homeland and streamed onto the dry prairies. They squatted on any open property they could find and filled towns with more people than they could ever handle. Most towns were overwhelmed. Militias were formed. Skirmishes broke out.

All the while, the sun never let up. It pulsed even harder, beating the land, day after day, year after year. Water grew scarce. Ponds and lakes dried up. Many rivers shriveled to streams and then to dust. Fire swept across abandoned fields. People fled the drying prairie all together. They went into the cities surrounding the Great Lelawala Lakes. Eventually, the caked soil began to lift off into the air and swirl into twisting sheets that spun into thundering dust storms, choking everything in sight. In winter, the cold winds scoured the ground and left it like a hard scab for spring to peel off and summer to tear away. Those who remained—all dirt-eaters now—struggled to hold on. They were bolstered by a few years when rain came and the heat lifted, only to be scorched and scabbed again.

The final blow arrived with the dwindling of oil and other fossil fuels. When the prices of oil began to fluctuate wildly, shooting up and down but constantly rising, there were riots all over the Meshica Union as desperate and panicked people fought for limited resources.

The cities around the Great Lelawala Lakes, like Menominee and Chikowa along Lake Mashenomak, created armies to protect what supplies they had and to fight off the marauders who terrorized and looted them. The Meshica Union became increasingly fractured and cities became isolated from one another. Gas and diesel were finally outlawed. Possession was a capital crime. In the end, the union broke apart completely, and the largest cities along the Great Lelawala Lakes took up the role of managing themselves. They essentially became city-states that were ruled by authoritarian power. They built walls around their perimeters like ancient cities and medieval castles to keep out the undesirables.

As a result, many people turned to old religions and new. Many dirt-eaters, including Joe and his family, followed the teachings of a former itinerant worker turned prophet, Roy Neolin. A few years after the land dried up, Roy received a vision from the Goddess Virid who had created a new paradise in the heavens. Over the next year, he lived in a dugout and received messages. He wrote down all her words and his own thoughts in a book called the *Word of Virid*.

When he first started to create a community, however, the prophet ran into a little problem. The central message of Virid, he said, was "The way to paradise is to live without a trace." Unfortunately, followers took this too literally. They thought the best way to not leave a trace was to not exist at all. Consequently, there were mass suicides. Prophet Roy had to go back to his dugout and receive a new message. This time the message was more direct. "Heaven waits for the humble." After that, the suicides stopped. Followers lived simple and humble lives, all in order to conserve resources so they all could survive until Virid's return.

Chapter 10

During the following night, the wind kept nudging Joe's shoulder until he woke up. They were sleeping outside in a gully that felt like a shallow bowl on the flat barren land. Above him the night sky was full of stars. He leaned forward on his elbows and glanced at the pregnant girl to see if she was okay. She was balled up in her blanket like a cocoon, in exactly the same position she was before he fell asleep.

Despite the faint "shhhhh" of steady wind, the night was strangely quiet. The crickets had stopped chirping. Joe knew whenever crickets went silent it meant some kind of disturbance was in the air. That's when he noticed something else. He couldn't tell for sure, but he could've sworn the wind had a raspy sound to it. It was similar to the sound the wind made when a dust storm approached.

Joe flipped off his blanket and pulled on his boots. He scampered up the side of the shallow gully and gazed eastward. The stars in that direction were completely gone. The sky was black. That wasn't a good sign. But maybe his fears were unfounded. Maybe it was rain coming instead of dust. Chances of that were slim. Dust was far more common than rain. He licked his finger and held it up to the wind for a few seconds before he wiped it on his tongue. It tasted like dust all right.

He didn't know how much time he had, but he knew it might not be much. A dust storm moved with unpredictable speed. It was strong enough to scoop up chickens and sheep and even cows. Since the scrawny pregnant girl couldn't weigh much more than a goat, Joe was afraid she'd be swept up and carried way. He had to get to her before the storm hit.

He turned and ran back into the gully, but he didn't get very far. A sudden blast of wind shoved him to the ground. Flat on his face, he heard the wind whistling and screeching past his ears. When he lifted his head, he couldn't see the pregnant girl anymore. All the dust whirled and whipped into a blinding black blizzard. He thought for sure she'd gotten snatched up in the duster. The wind lashed at his face. He went to call out to her, but he didn't know what to say because he didn't know her name. And even if he did, his voice would've gotten lost in the snarling wind. Nevertheless, he had to find her.

The thick blowing air seemed hell-bent on prying him loose and hurling him away. He kept his belly pressed to the ground and clawed his way over to where he hoped the pregnant girl was. He groped around until he finally grabbed a hard lump shaking against the wind. It was the girl. She was still there. The blanket flapped around her, so he jammed it beneath her. Then he wrapped her in his arms and used his body to shield her from the whipping dust.

In the dark cocoon he made, the pregnant girl poked her head out like a little bird and coughed. Joe caught only a glimpse of her before he pulled the blanket over her again. The wind slammed against his back. He felt his body rocking and quivering. His throat clenched and he gasped for air. He buried his face in the blanket next to the girl's head to keep from breathing in any more dust. He could feel the grit on his teeth.

The horses, Lester and Sam, whinnied. For a very brief moment, Joe thought of charging out in the storm and un-tethering them so they could get away or at least so they wouldn't get tangled up and injured. But he knew better than to do that. The duster would sweep him up in a second, sandpaper him raw, and gag him with enough dirt to kill him. Besides, he couldn't leave the pregnant girl to fend for herself. He hoped the horses would survive.

Even though he breathed into the blanket, dust still sifted through the pores in the fabric. The inside of his nose itched and his tongue was coated with dirt. The pregnant girl coughed again and he covered her head with his arm this time to help keep the dust from getting to her and clogging her lungs even more. His own lungs burned, so he held his breath. He counted to sixty and then breathed slowly into the blanket. He prayed the storm would pass soon.

Finally the night quieted down. The wind faded to a hushed breeze. The last of the flying dust floated and settled quietly to the ground. The stars and moon came out again.

Joe peeled the blanket back from the top of the pregnant girl's head to see how she was doing. It was the first time he'd seen her without her hat on since they left home. In the moonlight, her yellow hair glowed. It was all he could see, really. He heard her breathing low and steady. He figured she was probably still sleeping. For a moment he simply listened to the comforting rhythm of her breaths, but then he became more aware of how truly close he was to her, close enough that he felt little strands of her hair brushing against his nose and cheeks. He could smell her hair's sweet and dirty fragrance.

He worried about her waking up and being alarmed by how close he was, so he gently eased his arms from around her and kicked through a drift of dust that ran up his backside. Stars graveled the black sky. Mounds of black dust shone in the moonlight. After he stood up, his lungs suddenly rattled and convulsed. He hacked up a thick wad of black mucus that he spit on the ground. When he looked around he realized he had bigger worries. The wagon was overturned and the bonnet torn off and blown away. He got a sick feeling when he realized all their supplies might've blown away.

He felt even worse when he saw Lester and Sam. Both horses were collapsed and caked in dust. Their tongues hung out and their eyes were goopy with dirt. They looked awful. Joe brushed them off the best he could. Hard chunks of plastered dust fell crumbling to the ground. He needed to get them water to drink, fast.

He ran to the overturned wagon, hoping some water was there, but nothing lay spilled in the immediate area. Nothing turned up when he dug through a nearby dust drift either. He was getting frantic now. Without water soon, Sam and Lester wouldn't hold on much longer. He searched the scoured land for any signs of the water buckets. He stumbled around, hunched over, zigzagging like a drunken man. He found some of their supplies strewn here and there, but he didn't bother picking them up. He'd have to get them later.

He scrambled farther and farther away until he almost gave up hope. Then he miraculously found the water bota, which was made from a dried cow stomach, and a few paces away he discovered one of the five-gallon buckets of water. He staggered back to the gully. The heavy bucket knocked against the side of his knee.

When he got to the horses, he gripped the plastic lid on the bucket. It made a cracking sound as it tore loose. He dunked the bota in the water and filled it. He squirted some water over the horses' heads before he wiggled the nozzle inside Sam's lips. The horse's nostrils flared as it gasped for air. Joe squeezed the bota until it was empty. Water dribbled out Sam's mouth.

"Come on, Sam," Joe pleaded.

Sam's purplish tongue slid out for a second to lick the moisture on his lips.

"That a boy," Joe said.

After he gave him another botaful of water, Joe did the same for Lester, who revived much quicker than Sam. Lester was moving his head as if just waking up. Joe sat back on his haunches and took a deep breath. He looked at the overturned wagon again. He didn't want to think about what they may have lost, but he couldn't help it after a startling thought hit him. He was afraid the bundle of diesel had flipped over and some of the precious fuel had leaked out the cap. Every drop was indispensable. He needed it all to get as much money as he could, enough to keep his family secure for as long as possible. Maybe forever.

At the overturned wagon, he crawled through the front window and pulled up the floorboards to the secret compartment. He didn't smell any fumes. The deerskins weren't damp. When he shook the bundle, he was happy to hear the diesel slosh inside.

After a while, the pregnant girl crawled out from beneath her blanket. She looked half alive. A tangle of hair was knotted around her face. She held her crushed hat in one hand. She lifted it up and scrunched it on her head, but she didn't get it on straight, and the hat was twisted to one side. She staggered toward him in the moonlight. When she got to within a few feet of him, she stopped with a jolt, as if she'd run into something. She coughed and retched. Her round belly seemed to rise into her chest and then drop down again.

"Are you okay?" Joe said.

He tried to touch her shoulders, but she stepped away. She stood there for a moment until she must've felt better. Then she walked past him and over to the horses. She knelt down slowly on both knees in front of Lester. She looked so small next to his big anvil-like head. She spread her tiny hands over his broad face and gently wiped the dirt from his ears and the dirty goop from his eyes. She slid her fingers into his gaping nostrils and scooped out the dirt and gunk blocking the passages. All the while, she kept murmuring something that Joe couldn't catch because of how whispery soft her voice was. In fact, he wasn't even sure they were actual words. It sounded more like mumbling than anything else. Whatever it was, it helped revive Sam. After she finished with him, she moved on to Lester. She cleaned him the same way, ears and eyes and nostrils, and made those soft murmuring sounds in his ears.

In the morning, they dug the wagon out, scooped the dust dunes out of the cab, and gathered all their scattered belongings. Joe tried to determine how much they had lost. They had only one bucket of water left, a few scraps of firewood, and a few jars of food that hadn't broken. He couldn't find his hat either. It was gone. Further searching turned up the bag of pinole. The sack of dried meat was nowhere to be found, nor was the fishing pole and bow and arrows. Luckily, the rifle still lay on the ground where he had fallen asleep the night before.

He couldn't imagine what would've happened if they hadn't found the gully to protect them. Out on the flat desolate land, the duster would've stripped them bare and choked them to death.

Joe decided they should stay in the gully for another day so Lester and Sam had more time to recuperate. It meant one less day in finding water, which the horses had already half-consumed. Joe filled the bota until it was bulging for him and the pregnant girl. Then he let the horses drink the rest. Later, he got the old map out of the rusty glove compartment. He wanted to see how close they were to the river and the bridge they needed to cross. The map was the one that Frank brought back from Chikowa. Joe unfolded it and found the faded black line for the road and the faded blue one for the river. He knew they had to be close.

Chapter 11

The next day was even hotter. Some kind of breeze might've been a nice reprieve. The air was as stagnant and stifling as the hayloft back home. Joe kept Lester and Sam moving at an easy pace so they wouldn't get exhausted. He stopped now and again and squirted water into their drooling mouths from the bota.

Up ahead in the heat waves, Joe thought he saw what looked like a farm, but it was all too blurry to know for sure. There appeared to be the shape of a barn along with a house and a thin wiggly tower that could've been a windmill.

Frank said to beware of mirages, so Joe reserved judgment until they got closer. He kept waiting for the mirage to go away. He blinked his eyes several times, but the image didn't disappear. Matter of fact, it seemed to grow clearer with each passing minute. Maybe it wasn't a mirage after all. Maybe it was the real thing. Joe got excited, especially for a chance to replenish their supplies.

He imagined fresh water from the windmill and a little family with homemade food that they'd graciously share.

When they finally got close enough, there was no mistaking it was a farm or what was left of one. Joe steered the wagon past a string of slanting fence posts, which were half-buried in mounds of dust that were carved with ripples made by the wind. The bodies of two dried-up cows stuck out of a drift. Their ribs had cracked through the brittle skin and their hipbones protruded like plow blades. The small house nearby didn't look much better. The walls and the roof were gashed with holes. Out back was a faltering windmill with no blades, and off to the side was a short building with a dust drift pushed against it. The place looked completely abandoned.

Joe couldn't help but think that this was what could happen to his family someday. It was just like Frank and Dad said—when the land was scorched to nothing but blowing dust and no amount of money could change it. However, this place was out in the middle of nowhere. Their farm was close to a river and a still-functioning town. It couldn't possibly shrivel up like this.

They moved on. By mid-afternoon, Joe dozed off, only to jolt awake and squint into the melting distance. He blinked and tried to focus. The sky and the burnt ground remained hazy. He didn't know what he was seeing, so he made his eyes go fuzzy to give them a rest, but that only made him doze off again. The next time he awoke, it took him a minute to realize the wagon had stopped and the girl wasn't in the cab with him.

When he finally saw her, she was standing out in front of the horses, staring over a lip of earth. A hot breeze blew her dress against the back of her stick legs.

Joe jumped out of the wagon, but the instant his feet hit the ground, his legs buckled and he fell. His muscles were so stiff and cramped from sitting in the wagon for hours and hours that they were basically useless. He tried to stand up, but his legs still felt rubbery. He swayed backward a little before he stumbled forward and landed on his knees again. This time he hobbled a few steps on his stumps and then fell flat on his face.

The girl stood there watching him flail about without even lifting a finger to help. He pushed himself up and stared at her.

"You could've given me a hand," he said.

He got to his feet slowly, just in case his legs decided to betray him again. Then she led him to the crumbling lip of earth. She pointed down a sheer six-foot drop to a smooth plane of moving water.

"Wow," Joe said.

They'd made it to the river, Joe thought. The other side was lined with small trees and pale grass. Along the bank were sandbars that rose above the smooth water like the white bellies of floating bodies. He looked up and down the river.

"I don't see any bridge," Joe said. "That's not good."

Somehow they had gotten off the road and veered up to the crest of this hill that had been carved away by the river. Where were they?

Back at the wagon, he got out the map and tried to figure out which direction they'd veered. The map showed the river bending sharply south of the bridge. Joe thought he would follow the river a while to see if it led to a sharp bend. If it didn't, they'd turn back the other way. There was no reason to panic. They were at the river now, and water was the most important thing they needed. They got back in the wagon and rode down the side of the hill to where the ground flattened out along the river.

Joe unhitched the horses and led them to the muddy water to drink. He grabbed the empty water bucket and slapped it down in the river. When it was full, he lugged it up to where the girl stood and set the bucket down beside her. He caught a whiff of his smell and realized he stunk, ripe and sour.

"We'll wait till the dirt settles to the bottom and then we can drink it."

In the meantime, he decided to wash and cool himself in the river. He stripped off his damp green shirt and brown pants and stood in only his undergarments, which consisted of a one-piece top and bottom. He felt the heat of the sun burning into the exposed skin on his arms and legs.

"You want to wash off?" he said to the girl. "It will do you good."

The pregnant girl crouched beside the water bucket like a little bird.

"I guess that's a no," he said. "Your loss."

At the edge of the river, he dipped his toes into the slow-moving water before he stepped in with both feet. He took a few steps out into the water where it deepened and swirled around the top of his ankles. He turned to look at the girl. His feet sank in the sandy bottom but then held firm.

"Watch this," he said.

He spread his arms out to his sides like a cross. Then he closed his eyes, tipped back on his heels, and fell straight backwards and smacked against the water. The river rushed over him, rolled him a bit in its current and then tried to bounce him back to the surface, but he held himself under as long as he could. The "ooooom" sound of the water played in his ears. He held his breath until he couldn't hold it a second longer. That's when he sprang forward, blasting out of the water. When he opened his eyes, he saw the girl standing at the river's edge. She jumped back.

"Aha!" he shouted. "I scared you."

She apparently wasn't amused because she turned her back on him and stomped up the bank where she sat beside the water bucket again.

"Ah, don't be mad," he said. "I was just having fun."

She grabbed the sides of her floppy hat and pulled it down tighter as if to say it wasn't funny.

"It was only a joke," Joe said.

She scraped at the ground with her fingers.

"Be that way, then."

He sat in the water and grabbed handfuls of sand from the bottom and used them to rub the grime and stink off his arms and legs. He glanced at the girl once more. Her head was tilted up a smidge as if watching him from beneath the brim of her hat. He decided to have a little more fun with her. He walked up the bank, stood in front of her, and shook his body like a dog. A spray of water flew off on her. She got him back, though. She snuck her little hand out and pinched his big toe.

"Yow!" Joe yelped, and then laughed. "You got me."

After Joe sunned himself dry and put his clothes back on, they each took turns dipping the tin cup into the bucket of water and gulping it down. This was the best Joe had felt since they started, and he was beginning to appreciate what the girl had to offer. Before they left on their journey, he didn't think of her as contributing anything more than their cover story to throw off suspicion.

"You know," he said, "I don't know your name, like the name your mom and dad gave you. I'm kind of wondering what it is and if you could tell me."

He waited for a reply, but as usual, she didn't answer.

"What if I say a bunch of names and you nod your head when I get to the right one. Let's see. How about Becky, Susan, Rachel…"

He rattled off ten more but the girl never nodded her head.

"Okay," Joe said. "Well, why don't I make one up for you until you tell me otherwise?"

He pretended to be in deep thought. He scratched his chin, narrowed his eyes, and twisted his mouth until he came up with a name.

"Mary! How's that? I'll call you Mary."

She raked at the dirt between her feet and then dipped her knees in together.

"So Mary it is," he said. "Unless you tell me your real name."

At that moment, he happened to glance down the river at a stand of trees on the other side. What he saw made him do a double take. He saw a wispy stream of white smoke rising into the air above the treetops. He stood up and looked harder, squinting to make sure it was smoke and not something else.

"You see that?" He pointed toward the trees. "Somebody's over there."

The next thing he knew there was a rifle shot from over his shoulder. A puff of dust exploded about five feet in front of him. Joe whirled around and looked up at the hill.

"Get down," he said to Mary.

He hit the ground and scrambled over her body to shield her from another shot that he assumed was coming at any second. He crouched low and spied up the hill but he still couldn't see anything. His rifle was in the wagon cab. Trying to run for it was too risky, especially since it would leave Mary exposed.

Suddenly a man popped up over the hill like a jack-in-the-box. He pointed his rifle at them. Joe flinched and turned his head away in anticipation of another rifle report. When nothing happened, Joe peeked up the hill again.

The man was no longer aiming at them. On the contrary, he looked completely at ease. He held his rifle under one arm while he cupped his hands to his face and lit a pipe. After puffing on it, he shook the match out and flicked it away. He puffed some more. The smoke clouded his face for a moment. The man was short and scrawny with thin bandy legs. He looked akin to a half-starved elf—and he didn't look particularly frightening, either, but rather peculiar. His ragged clothes hung off him in tattered strips. Squashed on his head was a stovepipe hat. His straggly hair fell from the sides of his head like fringe. He didn't seem the least bit concerned or nervous. He acted as if he was all alone on that hill and he was simply enjoying a smoke without a care in the world.

He pulled the pipe from his mouth and shouted, "Good day," in a high gruff voice.

Joe sat up a little.

"I say good day to you," he said again. "Cat got your tongue?"

Joe got to his knees and stared at the man, still unsure of what to make of him.

"That shot was just to see if you were on your guard." He laughed. "Which you weren't. Could've killed you and robbed you blind. Never let your guard down."

The man walked down the hill in a bizarre way. His short bandy legs appeared to swivel out in front of his torso as if his top and bottom weren't connected right. His stovepipe hat wobbled on his head.

While Mary stayed curled in a tight ball behind him, Joe got to his feet. The man was a great deal shorter than Joe, but something about his gregarious nature made him seem larger. His skin was brown like clay and his cheeks shallow and streaked with hairs. A stringy billy-goat beard hung from his chin. He held his pipe clenched in his stained teeth when he smiled. His eyes gleamed.

"Nahum's the name," he said

He extended his hand, and as soon as Joe grasped it, the man's fingers clamped tight. He squeezed Joe's hand hard enough to make his bones grate together.

"Who do I have the pleasure of meeting?" Nahum said.

"Joe."

"Joe? That's it? Joe? Nothing else."

"Nope. Just Joe."

He could've kicked himself for saying his real name. Frank told him to never tell anyone, or else make up a phony name. But he was so taken aback by this strange man in the stovepipe hat that he couldn't think to make up a phony name for himself.

"Fine. Joe, it is. No need to be formal here." Nahum flicked his pipe to the other side of his mouth while still smiling.

"Who's that behind you?"

Joe nudged Mary with his heel.

"She's an orph—" He caught himself. "She's my girl. She's pregnant and I'm taking her to the city to give birth."

"Pregnant, huh? The city, huh?" Nahum narrowed his eyes suspiciously.

"Yes, sir."

"You sure she is okay?"

Joe looked at Mary. She still hadn't moved from the tight ball she was curled into.

"She's kind of afraid of people."

"Afraid? She looks downright petrified."

Joe bent down beside her, his hand on her shoulder, and lowered his head to where her ear was hidden by the brim of her hat.

"It's okay," he said, "you can get up."

He glanced up at Nahum who pursed his lips. He sucked hard on his pipe and then peeled open a corner of his mouth to let the smoke escape. Mary finally unrolled herself and stood up. Her head was bent so low it appeared as if it was growing out of her chest. At the full sight of her, Nahum stepped back and widened his eyes.

"Jumping Jehoshaphat," he said. "That tiny thing really is pregnant. She's about to pop."

"That's why she needs to get to the city. She's breech."

"Jumping Jehoshaphat."

"We need to find the bridge. We're off course."

"I'll say you are. The bridge is that way." Nahum pointed behind him over the hill. "My place is not too far from here. Why don't you come for something to eat? You look half starved."

A meal sounded good, and it would make the meager amount of food they had left last longer, hopefully until they got to the forest where he could hunt for something. Still, he wasn't sure it was worth the risk to go off with this very odd man.

"Don't trust me, huh?"

Nahum shoved his hand in his frayed pants, pulled out a handful of bullets, and flung them all into the river.

"Frisk me. No more ammo."

He held his arms out in invitation, but Joe didn't move.

"Here," Nahum said, "take the rifle."

He planted it right in Joe's chest.

"You got no more excuses."

Chapter 12

A while later, farther down the river from where they met Nahum, they arrived at a raft laid up on the bank. It was across the river from the trees where the smoke was rising. In the center of the river was a dry mud flat that shined like a dull sheet of tin as the water flowed around it in two thick channels.

"Can I make it across?" Joe said.

"Bring the horses and leave the wagon," he said. "Don't worry. Nothing is going to happen to it. You're the first person I've seen along here in a year."

"I can't take that chance."

Nahum waved his hand in the air with a dramatic flourish. "Drive on, then," he said.

Joe couldn't tell if Nahum was annoyed or if that was just the way he acted.

"I know a place to stash it," Nahum added.

They rode until they came to a rocky outcropping that stuck out of the ground near the river. That's where they left the wagon. Joe led the horses as they walked back to the raft, where Nahum heaved it into the water and used a pole to push himself across.

Joe looked at Mary and said, "We got to take the horses across, okay? So I got to help you up. I'm just going to lift you up. That's all."

The floppy hat nodded.

Joe scooped Mary up in his arms. He was surprised at how light her body felt, despite her big stomach and the child inside. He thought it would weigh her down more. Once he swung her up onto Lester's swayed back, she immediately tossed her leg over his neck and sat straddling him like she'd done it a thousand times before. That surprised him too, just like the way she took care of the horses after the duster. In truth, anything she did was a surprise, at least until he learned more about her.

Joe scrambled on the back of Sam and they waded slowly through the river. At its deepest point, the water only came to the horses' knees. Evening approached and the sun dropped lower, but the air was still hot. On the opposite shore they weaved through a cluster of trees until they came to a mound of patchy brown grass with a brick chimney sticking out. A stream of white smoke rose from the top. Behind the chimney was a rusty windmill that looked as if it might topple over any second.

"It's an old bunker from a long time ago," Nahum said, "when everybody thought the world was going to end."

He laughed and grabbed the black metal ring on the wooden hatch and yanked it open. They walked down a set of crumbling steps until they reached the floor of the bunker. It looked like a root cellar and certainly smelled like one. Musty and earthy. Above a wood table, a lone lamp hung from a rafter along the low ceiling. The lamp burned with a bright halo that quickly weakened before it reached into the bunker's dark corners. On the stovetop sat a steaming pot of what smelled like boiling fish. Joe stayed stooped over, keeping his head bent so he wouldn't bang it on a rafter. He felt like a mole in an underground burrow. And when he watched Nahum rummaging for cups and plates, the strange man sort of resembled a mole himself. His broad hands were like a mole's flippers, and his bearded face was like a whiskered snout.

Joe noticed Mary moving off to a dusky corner, where he was shocked to see a girl sitting there, her eyes wide and shining like a cat's eyes. In her arms she cradled a bundle. She rocked it gently back and forth. At first Joe wanted to warn Mary not to get too close, but then he realized she was probably drawn to the bundle swaying in the girl's arms. No doubt it was a baby.

Nahum finally found the plates and cups he was searching for and shouted, "Aha!" When he turned, he said, "Oh, yes. That's my girl. I named her Eileen, and that's her baby she's holding, and I named her Hannah, which was my mother's name. What do you think? Nice little family I got. She's mute, by the way. Had her tongue cut out. Shwack!"

Nahum stuck his tongue out and chopped his hand down in front of his mouth.

Joe stared at the mute girl.

"You want to see it?" Nahum said.

"What?"

"You want to see it, her cut-off tongue?"

Before Joe could really answer, Nahum walked over to the mute girl.

"Grab that lantern," he said.

Joe took down the lantern and handed it to Nahum. Then Nahum promptly seized the girl's hair, snapped her head backwards, and swung the lantern in front of her upturned face. Joe couldn't believe how roughly he was handling her. It was as if she was his livestock or something. Her big cat eyes were set into broad cheeks that tapered sharply to a tiny chin. Her skin was ruddy brown.

Nahum pried his fingers into her mouth and pulled it open.

"Take a look."

Joe peered into her gaping mouth. The glistening purple stub quivered in the back of her mouth.

"They cut it to the nub."

The mute girl pulled his hand away, and Nahum struck her with the back of his hand.

Joe was stunned. "What did you do that for?"

"It's the only thing they understand."

"But she's a girl."

"So?"

"You aren't supposed to hit a girl."

Nahum laughed.

"What idiotic dirt-eater religion are you?"

Joe didn't like the way he said that. "I'm a Viridian."

Nahum laughed even more.

"What's so funny?" Joe said.

"I can't believe people are still practicing that nonsense."

"It's not nonsense."

"Gibberish, then."

"'People will taunt you, but never be daunted.'"

"That's catchy."

"That's the Prophet Roy."

"Suicide Roy, you mean. Let me ask you this. Has anything the Prophet Roy said come true? Has the mighty Goddess saved you yet? When is the Goddess coming to rescue all of her dunder-headed worshipers?" He roared with laughter. "Tell me, I must know. Tell me. Tell me!"

"Stop laughing at me!" Joe shouted.

"The Goddess is coming! The Goddess is coming! The New Paradise has arrived! We're all saved!"

"Stop!" Joe shouted again.

He lunged recklessly at Nahum, who swiftly caught Joe by the throat and brandished a knife from beneath his ragged clothes. He stuck it in Joe's mouth. The cold blade pressed against his trembling tongue. He tasted the bitter metal and waited for the knife to jam through his throat. The lantern swung from the elbow of Nahum's outstretched arm.

"You got a lot to learn, kid," he said. "Everything is poppycock, and poppycock is everything."

He pulled the flat of the knife across Joe's tongue and out of his mouth.

"You're quite a fratchy one. You need to get a handle on that or it's going to get you killed."

Nahum let go of Joe's neck, and Joe rubbed it to ease the sting. He stretched his mouth and wiggled his tongue to make sure it was okay.

"You were making fun of me," Joe said.

"That's exactly what I'm talking about," Nahum said. "You got to learn when to keep your mouth shut if you know what's good for you."

"I was sticking up for what's right."

"Oh, idealism is dandy. But you're going into a different world now. Life is cheap. Take my Eileen, for example. I bought her off some tribesmen in the south forest. They'd murdered her family and had a sack full of their eyeballs that they'd cut out of their sockets. Nasty, brutish people. Avoid them if you can. Anyway, they had the girl but they were getting tired of her. They cut her tongue out to keep her quiet. They were more than happy to get rid of her. They had their fun, you know. She was damaged goods now. I was coming back from selling the horses I had because, you see, I was planning to never leave my bunker and to live straight off the land till I died. So, anyway, I saw this girl and saw an opportunity, a cheap one, mind you, to have a companion. I showed them a little money and they fairly threw the girl at me. But I should have known better after what they did to her. Let my desires get the best of me. She came up pregnant. A baby from one of those damn brutes. What can you do? They're mine now. Got to work twice as hard to feed everybody."

Nahum shook his head.

Joe felt sorry for the mute girl, but her story also made him think of Mary. After all, it involved an orphaned girl who was pregnant. He wondered again where Mary had come from and what happened to her. Was it possible that something similar happened to her? Had her family been killed? Had she been abused by some tribesmen? Was that how she got the baby?

"Eat!" Nahum shouted.

After replacing the lantern on the rafter, Nahum ladled out chunks of breadroot and strips of fish onto the tin plates spread on the table. The girls didn't seem interested in eating. Mary sat down beside the mute girl, who had unbuttoned the top of her dress so it fell open. She held the bundled baby up at an angle with one arm, propping its head against her chest, while Mary leaned over to get a closer look at the suckling baby.

"Who knows what kind of savage that thing is going to grow up to be? I should've dashed its head on a rock and tossed it in the river like I first thought I was going to do. But the girl seemed so attached to it. I couldn't bring myself to kill it. I got a soft heart, I guess. Who knows what kind of hell that's going to get me into? Dig in."

Nahum plunked himself down at the table and shoveled spoonfuls of food into his chomping mouth.

"How's it taste?"

"Good," Joe said. That was the truth.

"It's cactasil. I grow it in my garden near the well. It makes everything taste good."

When Joe finished his food, he brought a plateful over to Mary.

"You got to eat," he said.

She took the plate and scooped some up in the spoon and slipped it beneath the brim of her hat.

After supper, the burrow filled with a smoky haze that became so suffocating Joe had to open the hatch to let some air in and some smoke out. But it didn't seem to bother Nahum, who breathed smoke like others breathed air. At the mouth of the burrow, Joe sucked in the fresh night air and looked into the sky. It was teeming with glittering stars that appeared like falling snow caught in the glow of lantern light.

They had to get back to the wagon soon, he thought. He was worried about somebody finding it and stealing the diesel. Their bellies were stuffed, and they had two jugs of water and another empty bucket that Nahum gave them.

So when Nahum finally went to sleep, Joe and Mary snuck away.

Chapter 13

Through the night they traveled northward along the contours of the river. The banks glowed from the bright moonlight and the dark water shimmered. An edge of Mary's floppy hat glimmered from a bit of moonlight that shone into the cab. All was quiet except the creak of the wagon and the clip-clop of Lester and Sam's hooves.

Joe didn't want to spend the whole night in silence. He tried once again to get Mary to talk to him.

"How about that old man?" he said. "Kind of crazy, huh?"

What he really wanted to ask her was about Nahum's story. Was it anything like her story? Mary wouldn't answer, though, so there was no point in that.

"And how about that baby?"

Mary turned her head. That was all.

"You don't have to say anything right now," Joe said. "You can think about it for a while and then tell me later."

Near dawn they climbed a bluff studded with white rocks. It overlooked a valley where the river meandered off into the brightening sky. Joe could see some thin trees crowding the river's edge. He looked up river to see if he could discern a bridge, and he saw something dark that crossed the river. He didn't know if was a bridge or not, but whatever it was it led to some forlorn buildings on the other side. It appeared to be some kind of a town. His brother Frank hadn't said anything about a town, and neither had Nahum. Probably it was a ghost town, and not worth mentioning.

When they got closer, Joe had a hard time believing what he saw was the actual bridge. In the back of his mind he wondered if they'd somehow missed the real one. The present bridge wasn't much. It was made of wooden planks secured to rusty pontoons that stretched across sandbars and streams of slow moving water. He spotted some old tire tracks off to the side and some dark red shards of rusted metal. On the riverbank beside the wagon was a pile of crumbled concrete that must've been a pillar for a more substantial bridge in the past.

Joe flicked the reins. Lester and Sam stepped reluctantly on the shaky bridge and yanked the wagon up behind them. They plodded slowly while the bridge swayed and wobbled. Once they made it across, Joe could plainly see the remains of the old town—the half-crumbled buildings drifted with dirt and the wind-swept foundations of demolished houses. It was hard to tell what happened, or if what happened occurred all at once or in pieces. At one time, some people obviously tried to rebuild. They cleared the riverbanks of trees to construct crude structures. One of them even looked like a general store or a mercantile.

As they passed the second battered building, Joe thought he saw something move in its open doorway. He stopped the wagon and grabbed the Calvin rifle from underneath the bench. He stared at the dark doorway.

"You see anything?" he said to Mary. "I thought I saw something."

Nothing moved.

Then he remembered that stopping for the caravan had got him in trouble last time. He didn't want to make that mistake again. With one hand on the rifle, he shook the reins to keep going. Just as the wagon lurched forward, a half-naked man sprang wildly from the doorway.

He charged toward the wagon. Joe didn't have time to think, or else he would've shouted "Yah!" and Lester and Sam would've started to run, especially since they flinched and seemed ready to run anyway. But once again, Joe stayed put. Only this time he raised the rifle and aimed it at the crazed man barreling at him.

"Stop!" Joe shouted.

"Stop!" the man wailed back, but kept coming, waving his arms.

"Stop!" Joe shouted again.

The man didn't stop, though. He looked savage, like a rabid animal.

"I'll shoot," Joe said.

The man's eyes were wild, panic-stricken. He kept storming forward as if he wanted to attack them. In a spilt-second Joe pulled the trigger. He didn't even really think about it before he did it. For an instant, nothing seemed to happen. The rifle fired, then nothing. After Mary screamed, the wild man stopped short like he either forgot something or he finally understood what Joe had been shouting. Then his head snapped back, his shoulders twisted to the side, and his body crumpled to the ground. He rolled over twice and lay still with his face up. He was covered in dust. There was a black hole through his left eye. Joe had shot him. He looked at Mary, who was crouched on the bench, and then he stared at the dead man again. Blood ran from his blown-out eye. Beneath his head was a spreading pool of dark red that shined like oil. Joe didn't know what to do next. He'd never shot anyone before.

A second later, he noticed Mary standing in front of the wagon. He jumped out.

"Stay back," Joe said.

He cocked the lever on the Calvin, and as he moved toward the dead man, he kept the muzzle pointed at the dark doorway, just in case there were more crazed people inside ready to charge out. When he reached the dead man, he felt something behind him. He turned his head to find Mary at his elbow.

"What did I tell you?" Joe said. "Stay back. Now go in the cab while I check everything out."

Mary didn't move, so he escorted her to the cab and told her to get in and stay put. She listened this time. After he walked past the dead man, he glanced over his shoulder to make sure Mary was still there. He tried not to look at the pool of blood and the black hole where the man's eye once was. Joe was beginning to think he'd done the wrong thing.

When he got to the door, he already smelled the rotten stink. It was so vile he turned his head away for a moment. And as he stepped up into the doorway, he heard the sound of swarming flies. The stench was even worse now. Joe fought back the sour vomit rising in his stomach. He shuffled carefully across the dusty floor until he reached what was causing the smell and the swarming flies. In the corner sat the two dead bodies of a dismembered woman and child. Maggots crawled in their eye sockets and filled their purple mouths and squirmed in the long slits across their necks. The bones of their hacked-off limbs sat in a pile beside them.

Joe turned quickly and hurried out the door. He stood for a minute to regain his composure. He stared at the dead man. Joe reckoned he must've gone mad from killing his family and then eating their flesh. Maybe the man only wanted help or to be rescued. Maybe Joe had done him a favor by putting him out of his misery.

Joe walked to the wagon, got in the cab, and stashed the rifle below the bench. He was about to go when he thought better of it. He couldn't just leave the situation the way it stood. He had to do the only right thing he could do now. He turned to Mary and told her what he'd witnessed.

"We got to bury them," he said.

Behind the building, they gathered broken bricks from all the rubble. They made outlines of three rectangles of diminishing size. Joe retrieved the man he'd shot. He grabbed his ankles and dragged him. His outstretched arms rose above his head, and his hands came together like a steeple in the blood. Joe dragged him into the biggest rectangle and positioned his arms next to his body. He told Mary to start stacking broken bricks on him.

Meanwhile, Joe returned to the wagon and pulled out a blanket that he took into the building. He held the blanket to his nose until he got to the rotten bodies. He draped the blanket over the mutilated child. Flies whizzed around Joe's head. They buzzed in his ears and stuck to his face, but he ignored them. He tucked the blanket around the child's torso and scooped him up in his arms. A few maggots spilled out the end onto the floor where they writhed around as if in agony. Joe carried the dead child to its grave. He knelt down beside the toothed outline and rolled the body from the blanket. Mary stopped burying the man and stared at the child's corpse for a little bit before she continued to gather chunks of broken bricks again.

Joe used the blanket to carry the woman to her grave too. Like the child, he shrouded her body and wrapped her in the blanket before he carted her to her final resting place, still cloaked in the blanket. When Mary saw the dead woman next to the dead man—husband and wife, mother and father—she knelt down and bowed her head. Joe figured she was offering a prayer, which he thought was a good thing to do. After he said a few words to the Goddess Virid, they both spent the remainder of the morning piling rubble on the dead bodies. By early afternoon, with the sun blazing like liquid in the sky, they finished covering the dead.

Hot and tired, Joe drove the wagon back to the river. He unhitched the horses to wander out on the sandbars and get a drink. He and Mary splashed water on their faces and stuck their sore feet in the murky water. Later, Joe rounded up the horses so they could continue on their journey to the forest. He didn't want to spend the night in that wasted ghost town where he killed a man so desperate he ate his own family. It was a bad omen. At dusk, he couldn't even see the town anymore against the bloody sun sinking over the deserted plains.

Chapter 14

They found a place to camp among some scrub trees. Joe was exhausted. He hadn't slept for nearly two days. Despite the stifling heat, Mary had fallen asleep in the cab again, but once they stopped she jumped to work. She watered the horses and got the food and blankets ready while Joe made a fire.

His mind was still troubled with the fact that he'd killed a man. He wished Frank was there to talk to. Even though he had already asked Virid to forgive him, he still couldn't come to peace with what he'd done. Perhaps Frank was right. Perhaps this whole adventure was a huge mistake, a fool's errand. But he didn't like thinking that way. He didn't like the doubts creeping in like a bad disease.

Joe was homesick. He began to miss Frank a lot, particularly since they spent nearly all their days together back home. They did chores, hunted, checked traps, and kept Mom and Dad's spirits up. He missed the way they bickered and argued and how he could get Frank to laugh even when Frank didn't want to. He wondered how Frank was getting along without him and how Mom and Dad were faring under the stress of finding out their youngest son and the pregnant girl were gone. Not only gone but off on a journey his parents would think was treacherous and bound to end in tragedy. He hoped Mom's sickness hadn't gotten worse because of their disappearance. He knew she was probably bed-ridden, mumbling, "my lambs, my lambs," over and over. He also knew Dad must've gotten all bent out of shape at first and declared that he would bring them back. Without the horses, though, there was no way he could do that. Joe knew they were all worried and fretting. A part of him felt bad about that.

Even so, he was still convinced he was doing the right thing. They'd all be better off in the end. With the money he got from selling the diesel they could buy what they needed to stay on the farm instead of being forced off the land and into the city. There was no other choice really. No room to fail. He had to return home with the money.

After they ate that night, they both curled up in their blankets. In the night, Joe awoke and found Mary sitting straight up, shivering. He crawled next to her.

"I'm scared," she said.

It was only the second time she'd spoken, but just like the first time, Joe was astonished. She'd only said two words, but two words that added up to a lot. He tried not to make too big of a deal out of it.

"Don't be scared," he said. "We'll be alright." He tried to think of something to reassure her. "Remember, Virid is always leading us to what is true. She wouldn't lead us astray."

He figured that was the end of it. He didn't expect her to say anything more, but she spoke again.

"She punishes the wicked," Mary said.

Joe thought that was a strange response because he didn't say anything along those lines. Not even remotely.

When Mary spread her hands over her belly, Joe realized what she must've meant. She meant herself. She was wicked. She should be punished for whatever happened to her.

"That's not true," Joe said. "Virid forgives all sins if you trust her. That's what the prophet tells us. Everything else is washed clean, clean as snow, white as sheep's wool."

"White as sheep's wool," she repeated.

"That's right. White as sheep's wool."

Joe wanted to put his arm around her, but he still didn't want to do anything she'd take the wrong way, so he refrained from that small gesture. He still couldn't believe they'd had an actual conversation, an actual back and forth. He wanted to find out even more about her now. Why she thought she should be punished? How she got that baby? Where she came from? Who she was? But once again he didn't feel right asking something like that. Besides, she wouldn't tell him anyway. At least not yet. So he thought he would try to find out what her actual name was again.

"I know I've been calling you Mary," he said. "But I know it's not your real name, and I'd really like to call you by your proper name, the one you were born with, you know?"

"Mary," she said, quickly.

"Mary? Really?" He was skeptical. "I just made that up."

"It's Mary," she said again.

73

"I don't believe you"

"It's Mary now."

"So that's not your real name, the one your mom and dad gave you?"

"That name is gone."

"But what was it?"

"It's gone. I'm Mary now."

"You don't want your other name anymore? Is that it?"

She nodded her head.

When Joe spoke again, he chose his words carefully, which he didn't always do, but now he wanted to make sure he understood her reasons for wanting her new name over her old one.

"Because of bad memories?" he said. "Because you don't want to think about that person? You're a different person now. Is that it?"

"I'm a new person now," she said.

"That's right," Joe said. He paused a moment. He was starting to understand her more. "You can rest against me," he said. "It's okay."

She hesitated at first. Then she gently leaned her head against his shoulder. The contact was so light that Joe barely noticed it, yet its effect was more than noticeable. The touch of her head felt wonderfully soothing, as if she was trying to comfort him instead of the other way around. *Mary*, he said to himself. The fact that she didn't want her old name anymore, but wanted the name he gave her instead, said a lot about what her old life must've been like and how much being with Joe represented something better. It was hard to believe that being robbed, shot at, and killing a man was better, but maybe that was beside the point. Maybe what mattered more was someone being good to her.

Chapter 15

The following evening they camped a few miles outside of the forest. They had enough daylight to make it in and camp there, but Joe didn't want their first experience in the forest to be at night. Traveling during the day would be much better. That way they could get used to it and know what to expect. It seemed like the smart thing to do. He remembered what Frank said: "Don't be a hero. Play it safe. Listen to your gut. If you feel afraid, then be afraid."

They didn't make a fire because Joe didn't want to attract any attention. No one was around in the immediate area—no camps, no fires, no shacks, no shantytowns. The only thing that concerned him was far to the north where he saw white specks of light and glowing green capsules. The lights were from a biofuel refinery and the green capsules were giant tubes of algae used to make fuel and plastics. Of course, Joe didn't know that. He also didn't know they belonged to the city of Chikowa, or that the refinery and surrounding fields were heavily fortified with high fences, guard towers, and constant armed patrols.

Frank never told him why going north was the best way to get into the city. He only said that few people used it. Only the Hickabas from the cold regions far up north came stampeding across this barren landscape to raid forest dwellers and harass Chikowa's military. He wondered if the lights and green capsules were coming from one of the Hickabas' cities. It was probably why no one lived here. Whatever homestead was established would be razed by the Hickabas in short order.

They drank the last of the water they had and gobbled up the remaining jars of food. The horses chomped at the dry grass. He had to find some food in the forest tomorrow, but with only nine bullets left, he couldn't waste any shots.

They lay down on the blankets spread near the wagon, and Joe stared up at the stars that looked like scattered bits of crushed glass. He gazed at the moon. There was no use in pretending he wasn't afraid because he was, pure and simple. Going into the forest was what he'd feared from the very start, but he'd put it out of his mind to focus on getting across the plains. There was no escaping it now. From what Frank had experienced in the forest—the cold, the dark, the thieves, the refugees in rags, the violence—Joe knew this could be the most threatening part.

"You ever been in the forest before?" he asked Mary. In retrospect he thought that was a stupid question to ask. He'd only asked because he was nervous and wanted to talk about it. "Of course, you haven't. The longest journey you've been on is probably when you came to our place."

He got out his recorder, put it together, and played a song. He blew softly into the mouthpiece, just a whisper, so the sound was hushed like a sigh. He played a verse and then sang a verse.

> "I know dark clouds will gather 'round me,
> I know my way is rough and steep,
> But golden fields lie out before me,
> Where Virid's lambs their safety keeps."

When he finished, he sang a lullaby to help Mary go to sleep. She was most likely scared like him, so he wanted to soothe her mind and let her know he wouldn't let anything bad happen to her.

> "Sleep my child and stars attend thee,
> All through the night
> The moon its silver light will send thee,
> All through the night
> Soft the drowsy darkness creeping,
> Hill and dale in slumber sleeping
> I my loved ones' vigil keeping,
> All through the night."

During the night, Joe awoke suddenly. He felt as if someone had jabbed him in the shoulder. He grabbed the Calvin rifle beside his leg and twisted his head one way and then the other, trying to peer into the darkness to see if anyone was there. Mary's head was resting on his chest, which surprised him. She must've been afraid and moved closer to him to feel safer, to take comfort in his warmth and the sound of his heart. She seemed like a child to him at that moment, although there was something else there that he couldn't define yet. He gently squirmed out from beneath her and crept around the wagon. He stared across the dark surface of the swaying land. He searched the darkness for anything that seemed strange, not that he would know, because it all seemed strange.

After a while, when he was satisfied that his imagination was making the darkness come alive and it was only a dream that had stirred him, he returned to Mary. But he barely slept the rest of the night.

Chapter 16

Joe stopped the wagon in front of the entrance to the forest. The size of it was like nothing he'd ever set eyes on before. The tops of the looming trees rustled and shook in the wind like the clouds of a thunderstorm or the wave of an oncoming duster billowing across the plains. Joe felt at any moment that the rolling treetops were going to crash over him and send him tumbling away.

He flicked the reins and the wagon moved out of the sunlight into the dark forest depths. Everything became eerily silent, as if they had entered the belly of an animal, where the sounds of the outside world no longer existed. Dark tree trunks lined both sides of the road like giant stakes speared into the ground. Anything could be hiding behind them, waiting and watching. The wagon creaked and bumped over the rough road. Joe scanned the forest, trying to peer through the thick web and see what was hidden.

No more than a few miles in, the driver's side tire blew with a loud pop. The cab dropped abruptly to the left. Mary flew across the bench and crashed into Joe, which knocked him out the door. But he managed to twist his body in time to grab hold of the doorframe before falling onto the road. At the same instant, the horses reared up. They jerked the tilting wagon and took off running. Joe's legs smacked against the ground and flailed in the air. He didn't panic, though. Not even close. A few seconds later, when his legs fell against the road for a third time, he kicked his feet against the ground. His legs popped high and he hooked a knee over the edge of the wagon bed. From there he worked his body over enough to swing himself into the wagon.

Meanwhile, Mary caught the reins. She was doing everything she could to stop the horses. Joe crawled through the back window and toppled into the cab. He landed head first on the floorboards, where he curled around and scrambled onto the bench. Mary gripped the back of the bench with one hand as she bounced around. The reins were twisted tight around her other hand, all the way up to her elbow. They were pulling at her sleeve so much that Joe thought the coiled reins were going to rip the sleeve clean off her skin or yank her arm out of its socket. He lunged forward and snatched the taut reins at the end of her hand while he hung onto the dashboard to keep from bouncing out the front window.

"Get your arm out!" Joe shouted.

Mary shook her arm.

"Easy!" he shouted at the horses. "Easy!"

Finally, Lester started to slow, which made Sam calm down enough so that they both slowed to a trot.

"Whoa, boys. Whoa. Whoa."

When the horses came to a full stop—their heads shaking and nodding, their muscles twitching and shivering—Mary leapt out. She ran to the side of Lester's neck and spread her hands over his skin. She combed her fingers through his mane and pressed her cheek against him. His shivering muscles relaxed until there was barely a ripple. Joe watched in amazement until he noticed the rip in his pants and the red scrape alongside his knee. When he stepped out of the cab, his knees buckled under a jolt of pain. He hobbled over to the blown tire and knelt on his good knee.

The tire was shredded down to the rusty wheel rim. Joe had no idea what had happened. The tires were old and cracking, for sure, but for it to just blow like that was unusual. He looked back down the road and spotted what appeared to be a row of spikes sticking up like the tongs on a garden rake. It didn't take much to realize that someone had set a trap and sprung it just as the wagon rolled near it. And whoever set it must still be lurking in the trees somewhere. When he looked ahead at the horses, he didn't see Mary right away, and he jumped to his feet.

"Where are you?" he said. There was no answer.

He hurried around Lester and found her on the other side of Sam. She was stroking him and pressing her cheek against his flank.

"There you are. Why didn't you answer me?" he said, as if she was a regular chatterbox. "We're not safe. We need to get out of here. Get in the cab."

Mary stood there like she didn't understand, or else showing some kind of defiance. Whichever it was, Joe didn't care. He didn't have time for explanations. He grabbed her by her thin shoulders and spun her around. He shoved her to the cab and pushed her in.

On the other side of the wagon, he grabbed the rifle and quickly glanced into the murky forest. After that, he hauled the spare tire out of the wagon bed and dropped it on the ground. He could feel something about to happen, a presence, a portent, a static in the air.

Suddenly, wild whoops and cries shattered the air. Joe twisted around to see what it was. A stampede of men flew out of the dark forest like shrieking bats swooping out of a cave. They must be scavurchins. Joe had heard stories about them, about city wardens casting diseased, deformed, and homeless children out into the forest to die. Only they didn't die. They banded together into clans and survived. Some of them were especially vicious.

Whatever the men were, the men beat on shields and wielded clubs and machetes and spears. The terrifying racket scared Lester and Sam. They bolted down the road again, dragging the limping wagon behind them. He heard Mary scream. One of the wild men dropped to a knee, raised a bow, and slung an arrow at the horses. A hard plastic mask was pushed up on top of his head. He pulled another arrow from a quiver on his back and shot that one too. Then he slipped the mask over his face before he darted off toward the runaway wagon. A tail of hair swung behind him. His bare legs flashed.

For a moment, Joe stood stunned by the ferocity of the men's attack, almost in disbelief. They were akin to wild animals, covered in skins and furs and helmets. When Joe finally kicked into action, he flipped the Calvin rifle up to his shoulder. He steadied the sights on the man chasing the wagon. He zeroed in and fired. The man stumbled. He skidded to his knees, then crashed and rolled to a stop. That made the stampeding herd slow up, long enough for Joe to cock the Calvin again and shoot. The shot didn't go awry. The bullet ripped into one of the men's shoulders. It jerked him to one side as if gaffed, before he fell to the ground.

Joe swung the rifle back and forth across the dumbfounded herd of men to let them know that anyone of them could be the next to take a bullet. That's when Joe realized it wasn't really a whole herd of men at all, but only a ragtag assortment of about ten. Joe was expecting one of them to fire at him, but they all stood there staring at him as if they were waiting for someone to tell them what they should do next. They looked genuinely perplexed. Joe took the opportunity to take a sidelong glance down the road. He was relieved to see the wagon sitting there in the distance. Mary must have gotten control of it and they must be all right.

The man Joe hit in the shoulder writhed and groaned in pain. It was the only sound. When no one fired a gun, Joe assumed they didn't have any or maybe they did but they didn't have any bullets. Old guns were easy to find. Ammunition wasn't. Then a man in a red helmet lunged forward, wailing and swinging his machete, but no one took up the charge with him. The rest stayed still. When he realized he was all alone, the man stopped and looked behind him at the other men stuck in their places. He must've had a change of heart because he turned around and ran back to the group, wailing and thrashing his arms like there was something better in the other direction. At that point the whole pack of them turned and fled back into the forest. They left their wounded behind.

Joe sprinted along the road toward the wagon. As he passed the first man he shot lying in the ditch, he stopped. The man was sprawled out on his stomach, his head twisted toward Joe. His mask-covered face stared up in a way that made Joe feel uneasy. The white mask that circled his whole face made the man seem inhuman.

There was a little bump where his nose must've been and black and red stripes painted across the flat cheeks, but there was no mouth. The most disturbing part was the way the man's eyes stared out of the round holes. His eyes didn't move or blink. Joe stepped off the road and stood above the man. Blood bubbled from his neck. Joe still couldn't see the man as real, as a real human being. He seemed more like an otherworldly creature, especially with his white mask. Shooting him had felt more like shooting a beast.

Joe nudged the man with the tip of his rifle to see if he was still alive. His body was limp. Joe knelt down and pulled the arrows out of the quiver and peeled the fingers away from the bow he still grasped in his hand. Then Joe noticed a canteen on the other side of the man's hip. It was clipped onto the belt. Joe removed it and shook it. He heard water slosh and he slid the clip onto the waistband of his pants.

After he gathered up the arrows and the bow, he ran along the road again until he reached the wagon, where he found Mary standing beside Lester's rump. An arrow had pierced him and a trail of dark blood ran down his skin from the wound. Joe inspected it and saw that only the tip was embedded and no further. Fortunately, it was in a thick slab of muscle and hadn't hit Lester in a more vulnerable spot. Joe grabbed the base of the arrow right next to the wound and slowly twisted it. At the same time he gently pulled on it. Lester didn't like it. He stamped his hooves and shook his head. To calm him, Mary nuzzled his big head and caressed his cheeks. The arrow tip gradually emerged, forcing more blood to leak out of the wound, until the tip slid free. Joe wiped it on his pants and tossed the arrow into the bed of the wagon.

"He'll be alright," he said to Mary.

After they got in the wagon, he turned the horses around and they rode back to get the tire. The tilted wagon tottered along. When they got to where the skirmish happened, the man in the mask was gone from the ditch and the tire wasn't sitting in the road anymore. The groans of the injured man had vanished along with his body.

Joe was at a loss now. That tire was the only spare. The hobbling wagon would only put more strain on Lester and Sam, who were both showing signs of fatigue and weakness. Their tongues hung out and their heads drooped. Even so, there was no time to rest. They needed to get moving. Those wild men, scavurchins of some sort, were still nearby.

Chapter 17

They traveled on through the forest, which seemed to grow dimmer and dimmer by the minute. It was like they were sinking further into a hole they would never be able to get back out of. What Joe hated the most was that he couldn't see the sky. The cover of dark trees was relentless. At least back home the trees along the bluff were spaced far enough apart that light always got through. Plus the woods weren't that big anyway, not like here in the endless forest. Never seeing the sky was more disturbing than he realized. He was used to it hanging above him at all times, night and day, like a constant companion, a comforting friend.

Before nightfall, Joe spotted a narrow trail. He steered the wagon up into the trees for about a quarter of a mile and then weaved around the trunks until he was off the trail a ways and stopped. At first he sat there without moving. The tops of the trees hovered around them. The dark trunks staggered off someplace where it was all shadows. He watched the darkness spread like black oil. It seemed to crawl over his skin as if alive. He got out of the cab. The wind suddenly stirred. He listened to the scrape of leaves and the crackle of twigs until the wind vanished.

As they got the blankets out and spread them on the damp ground, Joe noticed how labored Mary's movements were. When she bent over or knelt down and then stood up straight again, she pressed her hands into her lower back, arching it, so her belly bulged out even more. He couldn't remember her acting that way before, or maybe he simply hadn't noticed. Maybe she had been moving around like that for a while, so it didn't seem unusual. In any case, he was very aware of it now. He wondered if she was in some kind of pain from lugging around a baby inside her all the time. Or maybe she got hurt when she was tossed around in the wagon cab when Lester and Sam ran away from the ambush.

"You sit down and rest a while," Joe said. "Curl up in the blankets and I'll take care of the rest, okay?"

Mary stood still and didn't say a word. Joe stared at her small figure, shadowed in the thickening darkness. He thought maybe she was too scared to answer him, or perhaps she was only being her usual non-responsive self.

"Okay. Stay standing if that's what you want, but let me do the rest."

He realized he was whispering. He wondered if Mary had picked up on that and now she was reluctant to make another sound.

"Everything is fine." He raised the level of his voice a bit, but then it felt as though he were shouting. Anything above a whisper sounded extremely loud. "We'll be safe. You'll see. We got a little water. Here—"

He grabbed the canteen he took from the dead man and unscrewed the cap. Before he gave it to her, he tested it first. He dribbled a little liquid into his palm before he dipped the tip of his tongue against his wet hand. It sure tasted like water.

"Only two swallows," Joe said. "The rest we got to give to Lester and Sam."

She reached out and slid her hand around the dented canteen and gulped two big swallows. Then he poured the rest of the water into a pot, along with what was left in the jug from Nahum, and gave it to Lester and Sam. They were so thirsty they nearly tore the pot out of his hands. He hoped they would come across a creek soon because they couldn't go much longer without water. He checked Lester's wound again. The small bottle of corn alcohol would've come in handy now to help disinfect it, but the alcohol was lost in the duster. The wound was as big around as the tip of his thumb, but it was clean and crusting over, so it looked like it would be okay. Mary stood close to Lester and stroked his broad neck. She went so far as to rest her head against his skin.

They didn't build a fire or eat that night. Joe was afraid to venture too far away, afraid to even scrounge something up like wild mushrooms. Staying close to the wagon at least felt safe. He changed out of his torn pants and into his spare pair. Then he wrapped himself in a blanket beside Mary. He felt her shivering, so he opened a wing of his blanket and gathered her next to him. She nestled under his arm with her head on his shoulder.

Once again he heard the leaves scraping together as another gust of wind cut through the treetops. It sounded like a whole other world out there that they couldn't get close to. He felt trapped in the forest, trapped under its black dome. But it felt good to have

Mary beside him. He liked how snug she fit under his arm and how the sharp bones in her shoulder seemed to soften against his body. She curled in tighter. Her hard round stomach squeezed onto his lap. All he could think about was making sure she felt secure.

"How do you feel?"

"Fine," she murmured.

"You sure? You're not feeling any pain anywhere? You're not hurt?"

"I'm fine."

They were quiet for a moment. The warmth of their bodies swaddled in the blanket created a comforting womb against the cold darkness. An owl hooted above them and Joe flinched. After a while the forlorn sound became more reassuring, like the owl was looking out for them in the otherwise eerie stillness.

He recalled the barn owl that made a nest in the hayloft back home. He checked the three baby chicks in the nest every day after the mother flew away to get food. One day he found one of the chicks had fallen from the nest and lay dead on the ground. Its mouth was wide open as if it died in mid-cry. Distraught over the death, Joe went to his brother Frank, who'd said, "It's only an owl."

"How's the baby?" Joe asked.

"It's asleep."

"Asleep? How do you know that?"

"It's not moving."

Joe paused. "What does it feel like, when it does move?"

"It feels funny."

"Funny in that your stomach feels funny, like you're sick?"

"No. Funny in that it's alive inside me."

"Alive inside you," he repeated, half-amazed and half-confirming it to himself.

"Sing," Mary said.

He felt her shiver. So he sang softly.

> "Sleep my child and stars attend thee,
> All through the night.
> I my loved ones' vigil keeping..."

He sang until her body relaxed and her head drooped under his chin. The darkness pressed in on them. He wished he could see the stars, just one, just one star shining brightly in the black sky. He knew it was childish to think, but he hoped somehow the dark leaves would open a space above them and he could catch a glimpse, a glimmer of one star. It would've been a comforting sight and made it easier to sleep.

Finally, Joe did close his eyes, after he said a little prayer to Virid to ensure that the morning would come without a disturbance and that Mary and the baby would never come to harm.

Chapter 18

The next morning Joe awoke at first light when the forest was still dusky but beginning to brighten. He noticed some specks of light sneaking through the thick canopy of leaves. Maybe that was a sign. He tried to follow one of the tiny beams up through the dense leaves to see if he could catch sight of the sky, but it was still impossible.

When he got up, his knee felt stiff, although not painful like when he had stood on it the other day. He shook it out, bending it and snapping it straight, until he felt it was in good shape. Maybe that was a sign too. He felt only good things ahead after yesterday. They still had a little bit of food left, but not enough to fill them up for one meal, so it was important that he hunt something down.

He grabbed the Calvin rifle and then stopped. If Frank was there, Joe knew he would say to use the bow and arrow to hunt with and save the bullets for protection, but Joe didn't want to risk missing a possible meal with the less reliable bow and arrow. Besides, he was a good shot. It would only take one bullet for a sure kill. So off he went with the rifle, traipsing into the trees for something to eat. He had a feeling that it wouldn't take long and he'd be back before Mary woke up.

After a while of seeing nothing but trees and fallen branches, he stopped and sat down to rest a minute. He was afraid he'd gotten his hopes up. If he didn't find something soon he would have to head back to the wagon. He'd already left Mary alone too long. If she awoke and he wasn't there, he was sure she would panic.

To his left he heard something rustle. He turned his head. The noise was less of a rustle now and more of a rutting sound. Then he saw it, a barrelback pig. He tried not to make the slightest sound as he rolled over gently on his side and then flat on his belly. He dug his elbows into the ground and leveled the rifle. The barrelback scuffed at the dirt with his snout and grunted like he was frustrated with whatever he was trying to dig up. But then it shuffled forward so its head was now in back of a tree, which only left his backside as a target. Joe thought about waiting for the pig to move again so he could get a head shot, but on second thought the pig might decide to wander off and he'd get no shot at all. He took a chance. He aimed for the leg. He hoped to crack it good and prevent the barrelback from running too fast too far. That way Joe could catch up with it and kill it with a shot in the brain. Right when he was about to shoot, he felt something touch his leg. He twisted his head enough to catch a glimpse of Mary kneeling behind him. He couldn't believe it.

When he turned again to the barrelback pig, it must've sensed something was amiss because it wasn't making a sound. It was ready to bolt, Joe thought. In his haste to get a shot off, he squeezed the trigger without lining up the sights properly. The pig squealed and ran. Joe jumped to his feet, cocked the Calvin, and went bounding over fallen branches and darting in between trees until he saw the pig again. It tore around the upturned roots of a fallen tree. Joe slowed down, raised the Calvin and fired, but the blast only bit a chunk of bark out of a tree. He stopped for a moment, panting, his nerves jittery, and then ran in the direction he'd last seen the pig. However, after hopping over a cluster of rocks, it was obvious the barrelback had gotten away. Joe was so frustrated he could've screamed.

He trudged back to Mary who was still sitting in the same place where she had startled him. She'd gathered a pile of mushrooms in the skirt of her dress.

"What's wrong with you!" he shouted. "I had a perfect shot on that pig before you scared it away. Now we got nothing, thanks to you. A bunch of stupid mushrooms aren't going to fill us up. But a whole pig would've."

Mary shook the mushrooms out on the ground and stood up. Then she did something that made Joe feel awful. She grabbed a branch and handed it to him, after which she turned her back and crouched low on the ground. She presented her curved back to him, expecting him to beat her with the branch for what she'd done wrong. Joe looked at the branch in his hand and then at Mary hunched over. He suddenly realized what cruelty she must have endured. No wonder she hardly spoke. No wonder she hid her face all the time. She didn't think she was worth anything to anyone. Joe flung the branch away in disgust. When it cracked against a tree, Mary flinched. Joe wiped his face with a quick swipe of his sleeve and sniffed.

"I'm sorry," Joe said. "It's not your fault. You didn't know. I didn't mean to yell at you."

He set the rifle against a tree and knelt down beside her. He laid his hand on her back. Her body twitched at his touch.

"I'm not going to hurt you," he said. He slid his hand along the hard bumps in her spine. "I would never hurt you. Never in a million years. You understand? We're in this together. You and me. I would never let anything bad happen to you. It's okay. I know people must've treated you bad before but I wouldn't do that. Never."

Mary finally stirred. She lifted her head and then straightened her back and slowly sat up.

"That's good," Joe said.

Below the sagging brim of her hat was a tear hanging from her chin.

"Everything's fine now," he said. "Let's get these mushrooms you found."

He picked them up until he had a handful. Mary pulled out the hem of her dress to make a basket for him and he dropped in the mushrooms. He split one open to make sure they weren't poisonous and saw the slender hollow space in the center.

"These are good ones," he said. "These are perfect."

On their way back to the wagon, they got lucky, but it was luck in which they would have to act fast. Draped over a tree limb was the limp carcass of a dwarf deer. Its throat was torn out, leaving a bloody gaping hole, and its stomach was ripped out too. Dried blood coated its thin legs. It was a kill belonging to some big cat. Maybe it was a panther of sorts who had dragged the kill up into the tree for safekeeping, which meant it must not be that far away. Joe had to work fast. He climbed up the tree, crawled out on the limb, and used his pocketknife to slice and saw off a hind leg before he jumped to the ground.

"Let's go," he said.

Mary shored up the ends of her dress around the mushrooms, bunching them against her belly, and ran with Joe as he cut through the trees with the Calvin in one hand and the deer leg in the other. When they got back to the wagon, he chucked the leg and the rifle in the cab while Mary unloaded the mushrooms in a pot. Then they quickly scooped the blankets together, tossed them in the wagon, and Joe hitched up Lester and Sam.

Once they were back on the road, Joe felt relatively safe again. They would have to wait a while before they found another good place to pull off the road where they could build a fire and cook the meat. The pot of mushrooms rattled on the bench next to Mary. From the corner of his eye, he saw her sneak her hand into the pot and take out a mushroom.

"You know," he said, "why don't we just eat those. Why don't you hand me some."

The road dipped, rose, and dipped again into a damp misty valley. Roots from the trees crowded the road and squirmed and bubbled across the slick rocky surface. Despite Joe's efforts to weave around them, the wagon bounced and bumbled. At one point, the tire rim caught on a knot and the wagon jerked to the side. Then the rim broke free and the wagon snapped back into alignment. Joe didn't like where they were at. He told Mary to hold the rifle in case anything came swooping out of the mist at them. Eventually the road began to ascend. They rose above the mist, which drifted away behind them like a cloud. The road smoothed out again, but Joe was still afraid to stop.

The mushrooms had barely put a dent in his hunger. His stomach growled. Then it dawned on him that they could eat the deer leg now. Why not? He reached down at his feet, clutched the leg by the ankle, and dragged it up to his face. He looked at the shiny purplish meat from where he'd severed the leg. He'd never eaten raw meat before, only cooked or dried, but what difference could it make? Animals ate raw all the time. If he was going to do it, though, he had to plunge in all the way. He thrust the raw meat into his face and chomped onto a chunk of rubbery wet muscle. He twisted the leg and pulled until the chunk ripped away. It tasted more gamey than what he was used to, but other than that, it didn't taste too bad. He chewed and ground the hunk of meat until it was soft and pulpy enough to swallow. He glanced at Mary. Her floppy hat was turned toward him, and he knew she was watching him, even though he couldn't see her eyes. He handed the leg to her and watched as she held it with both hands and gnawed at the raw meat.

Chapter 19

He heard what sounded like rain in the distance. The further they went along, the louder the rain sound grew until it seemed right on top of them. It had to be some kind of river, Joe thought, a fast-moving one with noisy rapids.

In time, they came to a small bridge made of blackened logs with a railing on each side. It spanned a deep narrow ravine or more like a gorge. Joe assumed the rushing river was down below somewhere. The bridge tilted slightly and didn't look all that safe to cross. The air was humid. The rain sound was more like a roar now. Joe got out of the cab and walked to the bridge.

What was most puzzling was how wet everything was, like after a long rain shower. The tree bark looked soaked. The road was coated in a glaze of moisture. Both Lester and Sam licked the damp stones and dirt to get any kind of water they could.

When Joe reached the edge of the bridge, he noticed patches of green and rust-colored moss scattered in the crevices between the logs. More patches dotted the bark on the railings. The bridge clearly wasn't meant for heavy loads, maybe a man and a horse at most. Certainly not two horses and a wagon, at least not at the same time, which made Joe wonder if there wasn't another way. He didn't remember seeing any other trails or roads splitting off into the forest. Maybe the bridge was sturdier than it appeared. He took a few steps onto it and rocked his body. The bridge didn't sway or creak. As a matter of fact, it seemed solid.

That's when he felt the faint touch of moisture on his face. He looked to his left, diagonally through the rocky sides of the gorge, where he saw a cloudy fog bubbling up from below. He leaned far over the railing, not even thinking whether or not it could hold him, and stared in wonder at what opened beyond the narrow walls of the gorge. White water spilled off a high ledge and plummeted into a steaming pool below. So that was the sound of rain. A waterfall. Of course. How stupid of him. The cool mist sprayed right against his face. He slid his tongue over his lips and tasted the mossy wetness. It tasted beautiful.

Then, without really thinking again, he scampered around the other end of the bridge where he saw a deep crevice running down the gorge wall. He thought he might be able to get a closer look from there. So he crashed through the debris littering the forest floor. He brushed by several trees and hopped over fallen branches.

When he got to the lip of the crevice, it looked like it would take him all the way down to the pool below. It wasn't a clear path, though. The crevice was full of sharp rocks, tangled roots, overhanging trees, and clumps of some kind of shrub. He scooted off the edge and immediately fell back on his butt before he went scuttling down the steep crevice. He bounced over crags, kicked rocks loose, and knocked branches and shrubs out of the way. All the while he built up so much momentum that he couldn't stop himself. He ended up tumbling down to the bottom and landing on a bed of smooth stones at the far end of the pool. He was a bit shaken up by the fall, but other than a sore butt and a few scrapes and bruises, he was all right.

Besides, in front of him, only a short distance away, was the waterfall crashing into the pool.

"Joe!"

He spun around. Halfway up the crevice, Mary sat slumped against a tree root.

"Joe!" she cried.

So much panic was in her voice that Joe panicked too. He thought maybe the wagon had been attacked again. He tore after her, stumbling and clambering over the rocks and twisted roots, until he reached her.

She held to a root with one hand and clutched her waist with the other. Her knees were skinned and her dress torn. She sniffled beneath her floppy hat.

"What's wrong?" Joe asked.

"You ran off," she said. "I thought you fell and you might be hurt."

Joe pushed her hat up and saw her whole face for the very first time. It was like a tiny bird's head stripped of skin and feathers down to the white bone. Her mouth was stained with dark blotches of dried blood from eating the deer leg. Her purplish lips quivered. Her eyelids drooped heavily over her eyes. Then she lifted her lashes and her wet eyes cleaved him like a wound. She threw her arms around his neck and curled her body tight against him.

"I'm okay," he said. "I'm sorry. I didn't mean to run off like that and scare you."

"I was afraid something happened to you."

"I'm sorry. That was a stupid thing to do."

His insides clenched as tight as a fist, clenched so tight he thought he was going to be sick.

After they climbed up the crevice, they made their way through the forest and over the bridge to the wagon. Joe had one thing on his mind. They had to get water soon. That was undeniable. Somehow he had to find a way to the waterfall. He drove the wagon onto the bridge, but Lester and Sam's hooves slipped on the slick logs. They stopped, unsteady and nervous. Joe got out in front and coaxed them forward. Their hooves clopped against the wood. The tire rim scraped along the length of a log, peeling off a black strip that revealed a line of yellow wood beneath.

Chapter 20

Once they made it safely across the bridge, Joe got back in the cab and they continued on slowly. He knew there had to be some way to the waterfall, and sure enough, just over a rise there was a track leading into the forest. The path was narrow and bumpy. It swerved abruptly one way before switching back. The wagon knocked against tree trunks jammed next to the path. A few trees craned low over the trail so that the horses had to duck and squeeze under them.

Then the wagon got stuck on something. The horses tugged and pulled, tearing off bark and branches, until the wagon broke away. Joe was afraid he'd made a bad decision. Perhaps this path didn't lead to the waterfall. But he had no choice other than to follow it to the end now. There was no way to turn around in the narrow confines. It was like creeping through a tunnel that you hoped held daylight at the end. The words of his brother

Frank echoed in his head: "Don't go too far off the road. The last thing you need to do is get lost."

Presently, they came to a fork. One way led up a steep incline while the other way dropped down a sharp slope. They took the slope down. The horses stepped slowly to keep from skittering over the rocks. The wagon rocked and clunked. Drops of water shook loose from the leaves and hit the cab's roof. Finally they reached a landing and stopped. For the first time since they entered the trail, Joe heard the sound of the waterfall again. It seemed to be blasting in his ears. Ahead of them through the trees he saw the white water and the milky clouds of mist.

"We made it," he said. "We made it. We're here."

Mary didn't move.

"Come on." He tugged her arm, but she still didn't move. He thought maybe she was still upset from earlier. "Just follow me, then."

He got out of the cab, and after he fought through the wet underbrush, he came to two trees leaning out over a ledge. He shimmied up one of the trees so he could get a better look at the waterfall and see how far the ledge dropped. As it turned out, the drop wasn't too much, and he would land only a few steps from where the edge of the pool lapped against the shore.

When he turned, Mary was standing at the base of the tree, holding a water bucket. In his excitement, he'd forgotten that the primary purpose of getting there was to replenish their water, especially for Lester and Sam. Joe hung from the tree trunk and then dropped to the stones. Up above, the white clouds of mist blotted out the forest and the sky. It made him feel as though they were in an enclosure, a warm, wet, misty enclosure.

Mary straddled the tree trunk and dropped the bucket. For the next half hour or more, Joe filled the bucket with several inches of water, so it wouldn't be too heavy, and lifted the bucket up for Mary to take to the horses.

After the horses drank their fill and they had enough water for themselves, Joe shouted to Mary, "Come on down."

She scooted along the trunk and then pushed off and fell into his arms. Her dress flew up and got trapped in his arms. When he let go she quickly yanked her dress back over her round naked belly. Joe made like he didn't notice.

"I'm going in the water," he said.

He stripped down to his undergarments and dashed into the water until he hit an abrupt drop-off. He kicked his feet against the deep water before he shot back to the surface again. He floated in the pool and stared up at where the waterfall crested the cliff and rained down in sheets. Whoever knew such places existed? He watched Mary crouch at the pool's shore, scoop up water, and rub it against her face.

Later, he got the arrows out of the wagon and they both walked to the stream running into the gorge. Joe waded into the swift-moving water and waited until he spotted a fish. They were hard to see because they blended in so well with the rocks below. He kept his eye on one, lifted the arrow above his head, and drove it into the water as hard as he could. But when he pulled the arrow out to see his catch, it was empty. He stood still and waited for the water to settle again and for the scattered fish to return. After he trained his eyes on another fish, he hurled the arrow once more. Nothing.

"This is impossible," he said.

He jabbed the arrow at yet another fish, but it too darted away. He flung the arrow onto the stones along the shore where Mary stood. Then he stomped out of the stream and plopped down. Mary moved and Joe glanced at her. She bent over her round belly, gathered up the hem of her dress, and tied it up between her skinny thighs.

"What do you think you're doing?"

She didn't answer, of course. She simply walked over to the arrow and picked it up.

"Oh, so you think you can do better, huh? Well, go ahead, be my guest. It's not as easy as it looks."

She walked out into the middle of the stream while Joe stood up and stepped closer.

"You have to be real still."

She leaned forward and hunched over. She got close to the surface and held the arrow above her head with two hands. Slowly she inched the tip of the arrow down. She hesitated, waited, and then jammed the arrow into the water. When she yanked it back out, there was a wriggling fish impaled on the end.

Joe was dumbfounded and elated at the same time.

"Bring it here," he said. "I can't believe you got one."

He pulled the fish off. Watery blood seeped from where it had been pierced. The fish squirmed and twisted.

"I'll get it ready," Mary said.

"Sure," Joe said. "I'll see if I can spear some more."

He exchanged the fish for the arrow and watched her turn and walk away. Her bare wet legs gleamed. Even though she proved more adept at spearing a fish than him, he didn't feel hurt by being outdone. He was impressed, instead.

After a few more failed efforts, Joe finally got the hang of it by doing what Mary had done. His efforts resulted in three more fish that he tossed on the shore to flop on the rocks. He found a pliable branch and strung the branch through the fishes' gills.

When he carried them back to the waterfall, he was surprised not to see Mary anywhere. He noticed a flicker of orange light coming from a corner beside the waterfall. It had to be an alcove. Joe figured Mary had started a fire inside it. Once he got close, he suddenly had a queasy feeling that something was wrong. He crept along the side until he got to the edge of the opening. He almost didn't want to look, but he did. He peeked around the corner into what appeared to be more of a cave than an alcove. When he saw Mary, safe and alone, he felt a wave of relief.

She bustled about like she was preparing her home for special guests to arrive for dinner. Preparing it special for him, he guessed. Over the fire was the cast iron skillet with the fish she caught frying inside. She'd spread a blanket out on the ground with plates set on it and an empty jar with some leafy green twigs and two blue flowers sticking out of it. Further back, she'd set up a bed of blankets for them to sleep on for the night. He was surprised by all she had done, and he couldn't help feeling a little swelling in his heart.

Joe smiled as he paraded in holding up the fish.

"Look," he said. "I got more. It's a feast now."

She took the branch strung with fish and slid them off into the hot skillet, where they smoked and sizzled. Then she grabbed a plate off the blanket and she pulled a blackened fish from the skillet and put it on the plate.

"For you," she said.

She held it out to him. He thought she meant for him to take it, but just as he started to reach for it, she whisked it away. She carried it over to the blanket and set it there before she placed a tin cup of water next to it.

She rearranged the flowers in the jar and then stood aside with her hand out-stretched, inviting him. Joe felt his skin flush.

As he ate, he looked around the little cave some more. Despite the wide mouth, the interior narrowed quickly into what looked like a tunnel. Off to the side, he noticed a pile of what looked like sticks. After he went to investigate, getting onto his hands and knees, he discovered that it was a pile of old fish bones. Some fishing line and hooks also lay nearby. Apparently, they weren't the first people to use this cave, and no doubt they wouldn't be the last.

When he returned to the blanket, Mary was sitting down. His plate had another blackened fish on it and hers had two. She had peeled back the skin on one and was tearing white chucks out to eat. He sat down again and looked at her and then looked at the two flowers between them. He turned his head and stared out the cave opening at the mist rising up from the pool where the waterfall hit.

"We can't stay here," he said.

Mary stopped eating. She wiped her fingers on her dirty dress.

"I'm sorry. I know you set all this up for us. But it's not safe. Other people have been here and they might come back. Besides, we should really stay with the wagon and horses. If something happens to them, we're through."

She didn't say anything. She simply stood up and began gathering up the blankets she'd made for a bed.

"We can finish eating, first," Joe said.

She dropped the blankets. He could tell she was upset.

As they ate, a part of him felt badly for denying her what she wanted. She'd made something special for them to share, a little home for the night, but the pleasure of experiencing that was gone. The harsh world took precedence again.

Chapter 21

The next day, they left the waterfall and continued on their way to the city. Near midday, a man on a huge black horse burst out of the trees onto the road. Joe stopped the wagon and reached for the Calvin rifle on the floor of the cab, only it wasn't there anymore. He'd stashed it in the forest last night, along with the bow and arrows. He kept the remaining five bullets in his pocket. He didn't want to lose them. Frank told him not to take any weapons, especially the rifle, into the city. It was illegal. If the guards found weapons on him they'd take them and torture Joe and Mary on top of it. Now he wished he had the Calvin.

Joe couldn't take his eyes off the black horse as it pranced around in a circle. Its coat gleamed like oil and its muscles rippled. The man atop the horse was dressed a navy blue shirt and shiny black pants with a red stripe down the seam. A black leather gorget covered his neck, shoulders and chest. He had the same red insignia for the Guardian Party on both the side of his helmet and on one of his sleeves: a seven-pointed red star with a white circle in the middle and a red bull's eye inside. It was the exact same one on the Arbyter they siphoned the diesel from. More importantly, it meant the city wasn't far away now. But that hardly fazed Joe at the moment.

He was more focused on the man on the horse, who was obviously some kind of soldier. Joe paid close attention to the rifle the man held. It was like no other rifle Joe had seen, but it looked like the kind Frank described as a S1 Corrector Assault Rifle. Frank said it could "spray" bullets and blow holes in a metal wall. Joe didn't know what to do. He was afraid that very "spray" of bullets would happen as soon as the soldier spotted them.

He grabbed Mary and pulled her across the bench beside him so he could shield her. As he did, he looked at the soldier, who stopped and stared at them as if he couldn't believe what he was seeing. Joe saw his face and was ready for the worst. When the soldier lifted his assault rifle, Joe closed his eyes. He twisted his body in front of Mary, but for some reason it seemed like he was moving incredibly slow, and by the time he covered Mary it would be too late.

"Move over! Move over!" the soldier shouted.

Joe opened his eyes and turned his head to see the soldier flicking his rifle tip toward the far side of the road.

"Move over! Move over!" he shouted again.

Joe quickly sat back, pulled the reins, and led the horses across the road into a shallow ditch away from the soldier. At the same time, gaunt-looking prisoners began to file out of the forest. They were all men, and they wore dirty yellow clothes, and against their shoulders they carried picks and shovels. A few of them glanced at the wagon, and Joe saw the hollowness in their eyes.

Several more soldiers, or more likely guards, emerged on horses leading more dreary prisoners. The prisoners marched in the ditch beside the road while the guards rode above them with rifles ready to fire.

Soon, the last prisoner came out of the forest, and behind him rode another guard who had a rope tied to the back of his saddle, which dragged something still hidden in the trees. The rope was taut and quivering. Seconds later, it yanked a naked man by the neck into the ditch.

"Don't look," Joe said to Mary.

He didn't know why he said that since she'd already seen worse, like those hacked-up bodies in that abandoned building on the plains. He even went so far as to shelter her eyes by pushing down the floppy brim of her hat. She was having none of it, though. She knocked his hand away as if to say he had no business doing that.

They both watched the body lurch and twist as it was heaved onto the road. The man's flesh was shredded with cuts and gashes. His arms and legs jerked and bounced.

Joe sat motionless in the wagon. What else was there to do? Mary still sat right next to him. He felt her arm against his thigh. While they waited for the horse to drag the shredded man out of sight, Joe wondered if that kind of gruesomeness was only an isolated incident or if it gave a clue as to what lay ahead in the city. Then he realized it was useless to speculate. It only caused doubt. He tamped down his meddling imagination in order to stay focused. No matter what, he was going to charge forward.

When the black horse was only a smudge in the distance, Joe flicked the reins. The wagon lurched and lumbered forward. Up ahead, through the tunnel of trees, he saw a slowly expanding hole of light, and through it was the city, Chikowa, the place they'd been traveling to all this time, the place they'd endured so much already to reach. He couldn't help but believe he was on the verge of fulfilling his mission of selling the diesel and getting the money his family needed to survive. They were that close now, just a little further.

PART TWO

CITY

Chapter 22

When they reached the edge of the hole in the forest, Joe stopped. The open gate to Chikowa loomed like a gaping maw beside brick pillars capped with turrets that shot above the treetops. Huge walls extended in both directions as far as Joe could see. He thought he'd be happy to finally reach the city, but instead he couldn't move. Even seeing the sky again didn't affect him. He hardly noticed. He couldn't shake the reins to get Lester and Sam to walk forward. It was as if he knew it was a mistake.

Ahead of them were rows of barbwire spiraling along both sides of the road. Joe pulled his pocketknife out and hid it beneath the bench. This could be it, he thought. The wagon limped out onto the road between the coils of barbwire. In the face of the towering walls, Joe felt like a tiny mouse creeping out into an open field where a giant hawk circled above.

Before they moved too far, an alarm wailed across the clearing. It startled Joe so much that he halted the wagon, which was the wrong thing to do. Several guards streamed out of the guardhouse bedside the open gate. And from the rear, an armored Arbyter rumbled onto the road and pivoted behind the barrier to face Joe and Mary. The gun mounted on top was pointed straight at them. The dark rectangle windows in the cab looked like the eyes of some kind of demonic beast. Even at a distance, Joe heard it make a low grumbling sound. The whole production seemed like a lot to put on for one tottering wagon and two spindly teenagers.

The alarm ceased wailing and a loudspeaker blared: "Proceed immediately!"

All the commotion made Joe even edgier. He shook the reins and they rolled ahead. The wagon hobbled to one side. Above the guardhouse door was a sign that read, "Security is Sacrifice," and off to the side stood two guards who held dogs. At the red and white barrier, Joe stopped the wagon. He hoped that was close enough. A couple of guards headed toward the wagon, one toward Joe's side and the other toward Mary's.

Joe felt his hand tighten on the reins and his face turn red. He thought for sure they'd take one look at him and know what he was hiding. It was all over his face. Thankfully, Mary did something very perceptive. She must've sensed how Joe felt. He didn't know how she knew, but she did, because the next thing he knew she kicked his ankle to distract him. At least that's how he read it. Why else would she've done it? When he looked at her, though, she just sat there like nothing happened.

"Holy cow, something stinks," the guard said.

Joe turned away from Mary. The guard crinkled up his nose and fanned his hand in front of his face. He stepped back a few feet. Joe was surprised to see how old the guard looked. The creases all over his face resembled an unfolded wad of crumpled paper. He wore a black helmet like the guards on the road and the same type of uniform, except his shirt was steel blue instead of navy and his gorget was brown. He also held an S1 Corrector Assault Rifle with a strap slung over his shoulder and the muzzle pointed at Joe's rib cage.

"What's your purpose?"

"My girl's breech," Joe said. "I need a hospital."

"Breech, eh?"

"Yes, sir."

"How old are you?"

"Eighteen."

"Bullshit. You got to be no more than fifteen. Kids always want to be older until they're old," he added, as if speaking to himself.

He motioned with his free hand at the guards holding the dogs and waved them forward. The dogs yelped and strained at their leashes as the guards led them alongside the wagon to the wood gate in back.

This was the moment of truth. The biggest test. Nothing could distract Joe right now. What if they sniffed out the diesel in the bundle? Last night he had gotten worried and scooped up some fresh excrement that Lester had dropped and smeared it all over the bundle of diesel until it stank. He hoped that would throw off any smell, but now he wondered if that would only make them more suspicious.

While the old guard continued to talk, Joe listened to the dogs' claws scraping on the wagon bed as they sniffed and rummaged around in what little was left back there.

"How do you plan to pay for a hospital?" the old guard said.

Joe didn't respond right away. He was too focused on the dogs behind him.

"I said, 'How do you plan to pay for a hospital?'"

"I have some money," Joe finally said.

Joe wished he hadn't said that. He wasn't thinking straight.

"Where's your folks?"

"PB got them. They're dead."

"You need to be inoculated."

A dog barked. Joe flinched. He thought for sure they were caught, especially when both dogs started barking. But then the guards seemed preoccupied. They looked toward the forest.

"Criminy," said the other guard who stood by Mary's window. He was much younger. It was the first time he spoke. "It's Fester," he said.

That's when Joe heard the creak and clank and clatter of some kind of wagon that must've been filled with junk. He also heard the faint yip-yip of a smaller dog. He was reluctant to look behind him because he didn't want to do anything to upset the guards.

"Is everything alright?" Joe said.

"It's just Fester," the old guard said. "A junk man. He comes through here about once a week. Thing is he has a disease that makes him shout insults at you, only—"

The young guard butted in. "Only I don't buy it. I think he just made up that disease so he can get away with calling us nasty names."

"Anyway," the old guard continued. "He's a pain in the ass."

Then someone spoke in sort of a high-pitched drawl. It must've been Fester. "Hi-dee-ho, boys." His greeting was friendly enough, but it was followed by a string of profanity. "Ass sniffing crap cans."

"Stop there!" the young guard shouted. "Wait your turn." He muttered something in disgust and stormed off. "I said, 'Stop,' you stupid scavvy."

"Hi-dee-ho, you ninny shit."

The clanging and clattering continued.

"Stop! I swear I'm going to shoot you one of these times."

"Calm down," the old guard said.

"But he's not obeying my authority. I'm within my rights to shoot him."

"Stand down, alright. You're getting all worked up over nothing."

Joe finally turned his head to the side and saw two mules plod past the old guard and stop. Sitting on the wagon seat was an old man who Joe assumed was Fester. He was dressed in mismatched colored clothes and had a muffler of matted fur around his neck. Perched on his head was a pointy hat with a droopy tip attached to a little bell. Next to him on the seat was a shaggy little dog that yipped uncontrollably like a deranged windup toy. The other dogs continued to bark just as madly in return.

"Get those dogs out of here!" the old guard shouted.

The handlers dragged the yelping dogs away to the guardhouse.

"Here to sell junk as usual," Fester said, then added, "maggot-pated jingle brains."

The young guard pointed his rifle at Fester.

"Get off of there," he demanded. "We're searching you and impounding that vehicle."

"Would you knock it off?" the old guard said.

"We've been letting him off too easy for too long."

Fester interjected. "Routine, routine, you manky wazzacks. It's all routine."

"I've had it with you," the young guard said.

"That's enough," the old guard said. "Go to lunch. Get. I'll take care of this. Go eat the pie your old lady made for you."

The young guard finally lowered his rifle and huffed toward the guardhouse, presumably to eat his pie.

Meanwhile, the old guard pulled a small hand-held device out of a pocket on his belt. The device had a lighted screen. Joe thought it might be a mobicom (Mobile Universal Communication-Information Device) or some type of scanner, the kinds Frank told him about. Fester stuck his arms out and peeled back his sleeve to reveal his wrist. The old guard held the device up and then tapped something on the screen.

"You're clear," he said and waved his hand for the barrier to rise.

As Fester clanked and rattled away, he hollered, "Toodle-doo, clod-noggin nut bucket."

The old guard turned back to Joe. "Now with that nonsense done, let's get this over with. Speak loudly and clearly."

He ran through a series of questions until he had all the information he needed. Joe tried to answer the questions as quickly as possible without sounding like he was in too much of a hurry. He didn't want the old guard to get suspicious and call the dogs back to finish the search. Joe knew they'd caught a lucky break when Fester arrived, and he didn't want that luck to run out too soon.

After the questions, the old guard pulled out a small box that he plugged into the scanner. A few seconds later, it spat out two silverish-black discs.

"Fasten these to your wrists," the old guard said. "They're temporary until you get to processing and get your permanent tags."

Joe took the temp-tags and put one on his wrist and the other on Mary's. He was so relieved that they'd made it through and so eager to get going that he didn't say "Thank you" to the old guard as they pulled away.

They were finally going into the city.

Chapter 23

Inside the gate, the wagon plunged into a dirt street crammed with ragged-clothed people and mule-drawn wagons and carts pulled by stooped men or children. To Joe, it felt as if they had been dropped into a pit of insects crawling and bumbling in every direction. Only they weren't insects, they were human beings. Barefoot children in rags and sacks scurried in between the congested traffic. Other children stared blankly into space. Scraggly women shouted and squatted and shuffled around. These people were all dregs.

A woman with the front of her dress torn open screamed at a group of men who were laughing at her. A legless man on a wooden cart propelled himself on his knuckles while children ran out and rapped him on his head with sticks. The man didn't even seem to notice. Then a girl in a frayed dress dashed in front of the horses. She raced along the side of the wagon next to Joe, followed by a scrum of shouting boys. Despite her grubby appearance, the girl's face beamed with joy. Her blonde hair fluttered behind her. Her skinny legs kicked up the hem of her dress. Above her head, she held a long squirming snake, as if taunting the boys with it, daring them to catch her and take it away.

For a moment, Joe couldn't get the sight of the blonde girl out of his head. The sheer delight on her face was startling in contrast to everything else. It made him wonder if Mary had ever been that way. She must've been at one time. She must've run like that blonde girl when she was a little kid. He imagined he was chasing Mary along the path that spilled out of the woods back home and led to the farm. He could hear her laughing ahead of him as he whooped and hollered, close on her heels. The scene was so vivid that he thought maybe it had really happened. Of course that was impossible. He'd never seen Mary until a few months ago. But there she was in what seemed like a memory. He couldn't get over how much she was laughing. When he was about to grab her and tumble into the dusty grass, he heard something crack. It puzzled him for a moment before he realized it was the crack of a horsewhip.

They passed a squeaky cart driven by a man with a shaggy mustache over his mouth. He snapped his whip as if he expected action, but dragging the cart was a single mule that plodded along slowly with its head down. Beneath the mule's thick collar was a circle of raw flesh. Joe's vision of Mary was long gone now.

Besides the swarm of filthy dregs, there was a wretched smell Joe couldn't get out of his nose—a smell of rottenness and feces and urine. It made his nose wrinkle. The stench came from ditches along the roadside full of mucky brown water strewn with trash and gunk. At one point there was a pump trying to force the muck somewhere else, but there was too much of it.

Packed alongside the ditches, one right after the other, were small hovels made of scrap wood, plastic, and rusty metal. The only difference between them was the color of the wood or plastic and whether or not a tattered sheet hung in the doorway.

Joe couldn't help but think that this grim existence awaited his family if he couldn't get money for the diesel. Even though Frank had described the slums many times, the reality never truly sank in until now, until he actually saw it with his own eyes. He'd never doubted Frank's word. It was just hard to imagine such squalor without seeing it. Although he knew their life on the farm was difficult, it was still nothing like this. But without the money from the diesel, they wouldn't be able to survive on their dying land, and the only option left would be the slums. It was better than starving. At least that's what Frank would say.

The wagon continued to totter and weave along the crowded dirt road. A train heaped with coal emerged out of the ground and slowly chugged above the mess of jagged roofs. Joe wasn't used to so much noise. Every sound seemed to ring right in his ears. They rode by a brick building that had a sign across it that read "Health & Rations." Dregs were pouring into the building with empty buckets and then pouring back out with buckets filled with sloshing water and what looked like some kind of root vegetable. Another building said "Day Labor Permits."

In the distance, beyond the chaotic slum, he saw black buildings and smokestacks cut against the sky like burnt tree trunks. Joe suddenly realized he could see the sky again. He hadn't really noticed before because his senses were too busy trying to filter through the barrage of new sights and sounds and smells.

After a while, they approached another brick wall that stretched in both directions. This wall, however, was much shorter than the one surrounding the entire city, and on top of it was a barbwire fence. They passed through another gate where they were quickly scanned, verified, and let through. In this new area, solar fields in shallow concrete basins ran along both sides of the road. Shiny square panels reflected the sun. On the other side were actual dirt streets with modest shacks and a single power line strung along poles. It was clearly a step up from being a dreg, even though there were still plenty of decrepit people around.

Eventually they reached two steel-girder bridges that crossed over a river. One bridge was for the train and the other was for the mass of people going back and forth from the city. Joe and Mary had to wait in line behind other wagons and carts that were being cleared through the checkpoint ahead. Going in the other direction, out of the city, were wagons full of dirty men, women, and even children. The whites of their eyes shined against their darkened faces. Most of them never looked up. Instead, their heads drooped and bobbed with the rhythm of the wagons. That could be him, Joe thought.

Chapter 24

At the checkpoint, a guard strode up to the window and said something odd to Joe. He said, "Visor down." Joe didn't understand. He was about to say "What?" when a pair of red-tinted goggles dropped over the guard's eyes from somewhere inside his helmet. Then dials encircling the red lenses spun around, back and forth, in quick jerks as if trying to focus. After the guard said, "Cleared," and the visor shot back inside his helmet, Joe reckoned it was some kind of scanning device.

Moments later, they were diverted into a fenced area where a bunch of wagons with horses, mules, and even a bisox were parked. More guards with dogs were roaming around and randomly checking wagons, so Joe parked as far away from them as possible in the hope that they wouldn't get to them. Even with the safe passage through the gate, Joe felt as if they had an aura of suspicion around them, as if the authorities could tell they were up to no good. He guessed as long as they had the diesel he was going to feel that way. He just had to accept it.

The parking lot was next to a huge building with thick pillars in front. It was the "Immunization and Verification Processing Center." Another guard steered them up the steps and into a large atrium with a vaulted ceiling. Painted on the wall directly in front of them was a gigantic Guardian symbol. Apparently they didn't want you to forget who ran things around there. They also didn't want you to forget that armed security was everywhere, and you needed to stay in your place. Below the symbol to the left was the word "men" in black lettering, and to the right was the word "women" in orange lettering. Thick black and orange arrows pointed down to a row of doors where people entered.

"Through those doors for sanitation and immunization," a guard said.

Joe turned to Mary. "You have to go over there. It's just a shower and delousing. That's what Frank said. And you know he doesn't lie. He said it was nothing to worry about."

She didn't budge.

"I have to go over here," he said.

When he moved away, she latched onto his sleeve.

"It's okay," he said. "I'll see you in a minute."

He led her over to a door beneath an orange arrow and pushed it open.

"Go in."

She hesitated. "You promise?" she asked.

"I promise. You'll be fine, and I'll be on the other side waiting for you."

After she finally went through the door, Joe hustled to the men's door. He wanted to get done as quickly as possible so he'd be waiting for Mary just like he promised. He stripped off his clothes and laid them on a conveyor belt that whisked them away. Then he went through a steamed-over glass door into a large shower room where he was sprayed with some kind of chemical. He wasn't expecting that, and he hoped it didn't alarm Mary when she got sprayed.

He hurried to a shower pod that immediately doused him with water before some brushes shot out of the wall and scrubbed him as the floor turned in a slow circle. When it was done, he raced through a heat blower that dried him and then he walked out the door. He quickly put on his clothes, which for some reason had a faint rotten egg smell to them. Finally, he burst into a dingy aqua-blue room. He hoped he had finished before Mary and she wasn't someplace else scared and confused. He waited anxiously for a few minutes until at last she appeared. He was happy, and a bit surprised, to see she'd made it through the process unscathed.

"See," he said, "what did I tell you?"

Yet another guard shuffled them into a long bright hall. Joe was stunned by the whiteness of everything—the walls, the floor, the ceiling, the chairs, the tables, the beds. Even the people working there were clad in white. The doctors wore long white coats and round mirrors on their foreheads. The nurses wore white dresses or pants and white hats with bright red crosses on them. All the whiteness stood out against the dingy groups of people being treated. On both sides of the hall were inoculation and examination stations. Some of them had white curtains drawn around them, while other stations were open for anyone to see.

What startled Joe was that some people were completely naked. An old woman with saggy flesh stood as a doctor looked at her backside. Joe realized that they were probably going to do the same to Mary, especially since she was pregnant. He didn't want her to suffer that kind of indignity, so he told himself he had to make sure the curtain was closed. If he had to he'd make a big ruckus and hopefully they'd be taken to an isolated place. If that meant a punishment for him, then so be it. It was the least he could do for her. Only then did he think about the possibility that the examination could reveal that Mary wasn't breech. But before he could dwell on it much, they were led away into an exam station where the nurse promptly closed the privacy curtain. That was easy.

The nurse turned out to be a very chipper and bubbly person.

"How are you two doing?" the nurse asked. She smiled and Joe noticed how white and straight her teeth were; they didn't look real. "Congrats on the baby. First time in the big city, huh?" She removed a scanner from her pocket. "Says here your baby is breech. That's an easy fix. We could probably do it here, but it's so darn busy we can only do things that can't wait. Like emergencies, you know? We'll get you set up with one of the public wards, probably number 3. There will be a wait, but there are some good people there."

The whole time she talked, she prepped everything for the immunization.

"Alright then, just a few pokes, a blood draw, and DNA for your veritags."

She was about to start with Mary when Joe stopped her and said that he would go first.

"What a gentleman," the nurse said.

He wanted Mary to see him go through it before her so she wouldn't be as scared. As it turned out, she was just fine. He, on the other hand, was the problem.

The nurse picked up the syringe, flicked it with her finger, and then positioned it so the needle was pointed at his shoulder. Joe watched it all, but at the very last second, as the needle drove toward his arm, he turned his head away and closed his eyes. The sting of the needle wasn't as bad as the burning sensation when she injected the vaccines. He looked at Mary to show her everything would be fine. Then the nurse pricked his finger, and it was even more painful than the shot. As much as he tried to hide that fact, his lip curled. It didn't help that Mary giggled, which he didn't think was very nice, especially since he went first for her sake.

He didn't hold it against her. When it was her turn, he told her not to worry and it would all be over soon.

The nurse helped too. She said, "Aren't you a pretty girl? You have such a glow, and I can see that pretty blonde hair hanging down from underneath your hat."

Joe expected Mary to flinch or cringe or make a sound like he had. He knew it had to hurt because it hurt him, but if it did, she didn't show the slightest sign. Likewise, she made no reaction when the nurse pricked her middle finger and drew a bubble of blood into a vial. Joe was amazed at how calmly she took the pain.

After the nurse finished, another guard led them into a crowded hall where people were lined up in front of six desks. On the wall behind them was the phrase "Security is Sacrifice" above yet another huge Guardian Party symbol. A row of guards stood below it. Many more roamed between the lines of people and directed them where to go. Some guards wore the visors with the red lenses. One guard, who didn't have a visor, poked Joe with the muzzle of his rifle and pointed to the far line. He grabbed Mary's bony hand and pulled her along. Ahead of them near the row of desks, Joe heard an occasional yelp and squeal. As they got closer, he saw people being injected with verification tags, a process that evidently caused some pain.

When it was their turn, they stepped up to the desk. The Verification Officer didn't even glance at them as he said, "Wrists."

With a pair of tweezers he tore the temp-tags off. The sound of them coming off was like the sound of ripping paper. What Joe didn't expect was the delayed pain. It felt like he had been singed with a hot coal. He flinched and pulled his arm back, but Mary hadn't moved a muscle.

"Remove your hat, miss," the VC said.

Joe turned to Mary. "Take off your hat, just for a second," he said.

"I don't have all day," the VC added.

Joe reached for her hat, but she yanked it off before he touched it. The VC held up a wand that scanned their faces with a crosshatch of tiny red beams. Then the wand flashed with two pops of light. Mary scrunched her hat back on. The VC tapped a screen and typed on a keyboard. Moments later he rattled off some questions that Joe had to answer hastily so as not to miss the next one.

"You have a three-day pass for the procedure and to make payment," he said. "If not, you'll be incarcerated until payment is rendered. Confirm?"

Three days wasn't a lot of time, but before Joe could even answer, the VC pulled a dispenser gun out of a holster beside the screen. The dispenser looked like a soldering iron; only instead of a red coil at the end of the iron there was a needle. Joe knew what was coming. He wasn't particularly looking forward to it, but it had to be done.

On the desk's surface were several vertical red stripes.

"Place your forearm on the red line," the VC said. "Palms up."

The instant they set their forearms down, steel clamps shot out of the desk and locked their arms in place. Joe was first to get a veritag. He braced himself for the poke of the needle, but the injection of the tiny translucent veritag wasn't as bad as he thought.

"Hardly felt it," he said and looked at Mary.

Afterwards, the VC ejected the used needle into a red basket and then pushed the dispenser gun back in the holster. When he pulled it out again, it had a fresh needle. He wasted no time in stabbing it into Mary's wrist. Once again, she didn't flinch. Not a single finger twitched or muscle vibrated. It was as if she didn't feel anything at all.

To complete their verification, the last thing the VC did was tattoo a code on their wrists above the veritag. He used a curved device that he pressed against their skin. For a few seconds something buzzed against Joe's wrist. It wasn't exactly painful. It was more like a sharp pressure, like pushing your hand against the rough bark of a tree. What the device left behind on their skin was a series of letters and numbers interrupted by a dash.

"Next," the VC said, and yawned.

A guard ushered them through a big door in the back corner. And just like that they were back in the lot where their wagon was parked. Joe looked at his wrist. Then he took Mary's arm and looked at hers. The code inscribed there was only three digits off from his, but somehow he was disappointed it wasn't the very next number. After he let go of her arm, he felt a different kind of disappointment, much worse. Seeing the code on her skin made him realize what he'd done by bringing her here.

Chapter 25

On the bridge going over the river, the tire rim on the wagon scraped along the strips of perforated steel. Down below, floating beside the riverbank, was a huge barge stacked with countless logs that men were chopping and sawing into smaller pieces. The dark river curved away and vanished into the vast city. The buildings directly on the other side got gradually bigger and bigger until tall buildings towered in the distance like mountains. That was the Green Zone, where they were forbidden to go. It was the place where wealthy business people lived along with government officials.

Finally they clunked off the bridge and hit a cracked and pitted cobblestone street that was clogged with more people. Some of these new people were dressed in better clothes. The men wore short hats with brims, and the women wore dresses that clung to their hips and fluttered around their knees. It was a whole new class of individuals mixed in with people draped in rags and barefoot kids scurrying through the traffic. A few of the well-dressed people held cloths to their mouths as if they were afraid of breathing in the air. One man had hoses attached to a small tank that was slung over his shoulder. The air smelled a little musty to Joe, like mud scooped out by the river back home, but it seemed fine in his lungs. Maybe there was something in the air he didn't know about, or maybe those people didn't like earthy smells.

He was amazed by how many people were jammed into the city. In the last few hours, he'd seen more people than he'd ever seen in his entire life. At the same time, it all became overwhelming, and Joe wanted to get away—away from the strange people, bicycles, horses, carts, pickup wagons, car buggies, and even some actual moving cars.

Joe had seen plenty of beat-up and patched-up old cars, but he'd never seen any that weren't pulled by horses or bisox. The three different cars he saw right then weren't very big. In fact, they didn't look like they could carry more than a few people. They had snub noses and bubble cabs and probably ran solely on electricity. Gas and diesel were only used for larger vehicles, like Arbyters, and for long-distance travel, especially since electricity didn't really exist outside the city.

To be honest, Joe didn't know where he was going. He knew where the steel mill was because Frank had sketched it on a scrap of paper, but that was a long ways away. What they needed to do was find a place to stay first. Focus on that, he thought. And worry about the rest later. So when he saw a corner, he turned down it. The noise of the main street faded. This narrower street was lined with grimy row houses, one after the other, with no space between them. It was a wall of dark brick on both sides like a canyon. Everything was dirty and dingy. Joe couldn't understand how anyone could live here. A few stunted trees dotted the edge of the street. On top of some of the roofs, chimneys coughed smoke.

After they passed a cross street, the buildings were broken up by tight passageways in between. The buildings had crumbling stoops leading down from dark doors to cracked sidewalks. One of them had a sign out front that read "Rooming House." Across the street, three rough-looking boys loitered on a stoop. They smoked cigarettes and stared at the wagon. Joe had a bad feeling about them, so he took Mary with him up the steps to the rooming house. Although that left the wagon unattended, he didn't want to leave Mary alone and risk her being harassed. Even if the ruffians snooped in the wagon, they wouldn't find the hidden bundle of diesel.

When he pushed open the door, a bell jingled, and they stepped onto a threadbare carpet. Joe nudged Mary forward and closed the door. Inside, the air was stuffy and humid. It smelled like an old leather shoe. A fat woman in a stained dress sat behind a desk. Her eyes fluttered but didn't open. She didn't seem to notice that a young boy and a pregnant girl stood in front of her. Thin tubes ran out of each of her nostrils and came together in a hose that rested on her bosom.

Joe was about to reach forward and tap the woman on her shoulder when a man came rushing out of a nearby room. The moment he saw them he stopped. He had a silver monocle like a small telescope strapped to one eye.

"Ah, guests," he said. "I'm the proprietor here. Welcome." He paused for a second, and Joe thought he was going to introduce the woman with the tubes, but he didn't. "I see your lady is with child," he said.

"That's why we've come here. My girl is breech and I need to take her to a hospital."

"A public ward will certainly take you. Sign in, please."

On the desk lay an open ledger with names and dates on it. Joe picked up a pencil attached to a dirty string and scribbled down his name and Mary's name in crude letters.

"Excellent," the proprietor said. He still had the monocle in his eye. "Wrists, please, so Mildred can scan your tags."

When Joe looked at the fat woman with the tubes in her nose, she was now alert and smiled at him. She held what looked like a small gun with a red strip of light at the end. She waved it over their wrists and then turned to a screen trimmed with engraved brass and started typing on a keyboard.

After the proprietor quoted the price, Joe dug in his pocket, pulled out the drawstring purse, and handed some coins to the man, who unfurled his long fingers and clenched the money. He stashed it on the inside of his coat and then ushered them upstairs to a room. Joe explained that he had a wagon and horses that he needed to stable somewhere.

"Splendid," the proprietor said. "There's a small stable out back."

When they went outside to the wagon, the three ruffians now stood in the street, not far from the wagon. Joe tried not to pay any attention to them. He helped Mary into the cab before he got in and drove the wagon around the sharp corner and down a tight passageway to the bricked-in backyard where a makeshift stable stood.

Inside the stable, he unhitched the horses and found some stale hay in a corner for Sam and Lester to munch on. Mary gave them some water from the buckets. After that, Joe wondered if they should even go in the rooming house. He thought maybe they should stay in the stable instead. He worried about the three young ruffians. He still didn't have a good feeling about them, and he thought perhaps it made more sense to stay with the wagon and the diesel. But then he considered how nice it would be for Mary to sleep in a proper bed. It didn't seem right to deny her that luxury, especially after they already paid for it. Plus, he kind of wanted to see how she would react. He was sure it would make her happy.

"You're going to sleep like a princess tonight," Joe said. "After all those nights on the plains and in the forest, you're finally going to sleep in a real bed. You won't know what to do with yourself. You might faint with happiness. You might not ever want to leave."

"Yes, I will," Mary said.

"I don't know. You might have it so good, you'll want to stay."

"Never."

"Never? How do you know yet? You haven't seen our room and the big soft bed."

"I'll miss Mom and Dad and Frank."

"I know," Joe said. "I was only teasing you."

He thought he saw her little chin twitch as if she were grinning behind the brim of her hat.

Chapter 26

When they got in the small room, Joe flipped the switch on the wall and the light bulb hanging from the ceiling flickered on and shone with a weak light.

"That's a light bulb," he said.

"I know," Mary said.

Joe assumed she'd never seen one, but apparently he was wrong. Or maybe she wanted to appear worldly and that's why she didn't even glance at the light bulb. She acted like she'd seen electric light a hundred times before. Well, Joe thought, if that didn't impress her then surely she'd be impressed by the magic of television. As it turned out, he was wrong about that too.

Of all the things he was curious to see in the city, like helicrafts for one, he was most intrigued by television. Joe had heard about it from Frank, but Joe had never seen one, at least not one that worked. His excitement made the fear he felt earlier in the stable seem to vanish.

"This is a television," he said. "I know you haven't seen one of those. You're going to be amazed."

He stood in front of the dresser where a small television sat. It was framed in wood with strips of embroidered brass on the outer corners. When he turned the television on, he was disappointed at first. The picture was a blizzard of black and white dots and only static came out of the speaker. He turned the channel several times until there was finally a picture. It seemed to pop out at him.

"Aha, look at that!"

He stepped back to get a better view. A woman with bright red lipstick stared at Joe. The view panned down her black dress and then showed an exposed white leg gleaming all the way to the floor. He didn't know what he had anticipated, but it wasn't that. On the next channel, a longhaired man in animal skins was racing a vehicle through a desert and fighting with another vehicle racing alongside him.

"Is this wild or what?" Joe said.

When he looked at Mary she had her head down.

"You aren't even looking."

The images were incredible. Joe could've sat and watched them some more. But Mary didn't seem to be the least bit interested. She was a strange girl. How could she not even look? Maybe she was afraid and that was why. He decided to show her the bathroom. He thought she might want to take a bath and relax. Back home, Mom often made a bath for her in the cracked porcelain tub. Frank and Dad weren't happy about it because they said it was a waste of water, but Mom said, "That girl needs pampering, and that's all that's to it." So Joe thought a bath might make her feel more at home.

The tile on the bathroom floor was chipped and cracked. Black mold ran along the seams. The inside of the toilet bowl was covered in a rusty-brown color. Next to the tiny sink was a curtain. When Joe pulled it open, it revealed a narrow tub-shower with a corroded nozzle and a rusty drain.

He reached in and turned the knobs. There was a squeak, then a rumble, and then a gurgling sound before the nozzle spit out some brown water. After that, the water began to clear and pattered in the tub with a feeble stream. He wasn't quite sure how to make the water come out of the spigot, so he just let the shower fill the tub.

When it was finished, he said, "There you go. A warm bath for you. I'll let you be and check on you later, okay?"

She didn't respond.

"I'll take that as a yes, then."

In the room, he turned on the television again and watched a man in a gray fedora smoking a cigarette in a bar. The man watched a woman dancing on a stage until another woman in a sleek dress sat down next to him and whispered something in his ear. He had sort of a half-smirk, half-grin on his face like he was amused and skeptical at the same time. His face was clean-shaven, although his skin looked a little weathered, while his eyes had a shimmer to them. Joe liked him right away. He could've watched him longer, but he was curious about what was on the other channels.

When he flipped to another channel, "Terror Alert" flashed across the top of the screen. Grainy video ran of what appeared to be the north gate they had passed through that morning, only it was under attack. The attackers wore black bandanas tied around their heads with some kind of yellow emblem on the front that Joe couldn't make out. The fighters shot rifles like Joe's and handguns and a few even fired assault rifles. They streamed out of the woods like black ants, flowing into the clearing and onto the road. They broke into the guardhouse and freed the prisoners.

Joe thought perhaps this was another movie until a voice spoke through the speaker. It said this was the second terror attack in the last three weeks and that it had happened that morning. Thankfully, city forces had successfully repelled the assault with swift, decisive, and valiant action. The screen showed the doors of a massive gate closing. Then an Arbyter mounted with cannons blasted shells. Airplanes swooped over the top of the city walls and strafed the attackers below. There was a close-up of a dead man on the ground. On his bandana was a yellow emblem of a coiled snake with its head up, ready to strike.

Joe was stunned by what he saw because he'd seen no such attack that morning. Everything had been peaceful. It had to be something from some other time, but in the lower left-hand corner of the screen was a date and time. He flipped to the other channels to see if they had dates, too, and each one had the exact same date.

When he returned to the channel with the attack, a man now stood in front of a banner with the ubiquitous Guardian symbol. The man's face was smooth and handsome. His slicked-back blond hair shone bright. He wore a crisp suit with a red tie. At the bottom of the screen, it read "Minister of Peace and Security." He explained that terror could strike at anytime. "It is ruthless and unpredictable. Terrorists are heartless and savage. They are avowed enemies to peace, freedom, and security." He went on to say, "Every citizen must remain steadfast and vigilant against agents of terror who live only to destroy what we have secured. It is therefore imperative to report any suspicious behavior to the authorities. Terror is insidious in its ability to infiltrate and mingle among lovers of peace. As always, 'Security is Freedom.'" That was the first time Joe had heard that slogan.

Joe turned the channel after that because the warning was making him nervous. Attacks on the city were no concern of his. He was here for one thing. Once he got the money for the diesel and got safely out of the city, it could all burn down as far as he was concerned. He found a channel with a huge steam-ship plowing through the ocean. On board were lots of people in fancy clothes parading around on deck and in a huge ballroom. Joe was fascinated by the whole spectacle. The opulence was more than he could fathom.

Moments later, Joe heard a popping sound from outside the window. He immediately thought of the diesel. He rushed to the window and threw open the curtain, but he couldn't see anything except the top of the stable. Below the sill was a slanting roof that blocked his view. A trace of light appeared from somewhere below. It flashed, wavered, and then went out. Joe didn't know what it was, but he wasn't going to wait to find out. Before he left, he knocked on the bathroom door and told Mary he was going to check the horses and wagon. He tried to make his voice sound as calm as possible so she wouldn't get worried or alarmed.

"I'll be right back," he said.

On the first floor he hurried back to the kitchen. At the table sat a man with a ring of whiskers around his mouth and a chubby woman with a face like a lumpy pie. When the woman looked up at Joe, he noticed a purple bruise beneath her left eye. She gave him a weak smile. The man grunted. He was gnawing on a bone and his fingers glistened with grease.

Outside in the stable, Joe turned a knob and a single light sputtered to life. No one was in there. Thank heavens. He checked the wagon and patted Lester and Sam. Everything seemed to be all right. He figured he got panicked for nothing. When he turned around, the three young ruffians from earlier were milling around the entrance to the stable. They smoked, whispered to each other, and eyed Joe and the wagon. The brims of their wool caps kept their eyes in shadows. All Joe could see were their mouths and the glowing red tips of their cigarettes. Joe tried to look busy. He fed the horses some more hay and checked their hooves, but then he didn't know what else to do. He didn't want to leave; yet he couldn't stand there all night.

As he left, one of them sneered, "Dirt-eater."

Back in the kitchen, only the man with a ring of whiskers was at the table.

"How do I keep my wagon safe?" Joe said.

"That's not my problem." The man looked Joe up and down, as if appraising him, and the appraisal didn't seem good. "What do you got that needs to be safe, anyway? You hiding something?"

"No."

"Then what's the big deal? Nobody wants anything of yours."

"But what about those men?"

"What men?"

"They were in the street when we got here and now they're in the stable."

"They're punks. They just want to scare you."

"But what is there to stop them?"

"What do you got that they want, anyway, kid? Why are you so worried? Do I need to report you?"

"No, sir."

Joe realized he was making the man even more suspicious. He thanked him and walked out.

In the front room, he found the proprietor sitting in a chair with an old telephone handset to his ear. The monocle was still fastened to his eye. He seemed to be listening very intently to something on the other end, although there was no cord attached to it.

When he saw Joe, he said, "Hold on," into the handset, and then to Joe he said, "Yes? What is it?"

"I was wondering if there was a way to lock the stable."

"Lock it? What for?"

"Well, there are three men in it."

"There is? Dang neighbors. I'll shoo them out in a minute."

"Can you lock it?"

"It doesn't have a lock. I'll tell those boys to go home in a minute. Don't worry."

But Joe did worry.

Chapter 27

When he got back to the room, Mary was lying on the bed, covered in a white sheet. Her yellow hair was wet and spread out on the pillow. It was the first time he had really gotten a good look at her without her hat on. He'd seen her face and the top of her head before, but never at the same time. Even when she removed her hat for the veritags, it didn't really count because he wasn't exactly looking at her.

At that moment, however, what he saw in front of him was the whole picture. He had meant to tell her about the young ruffians in the stable, but he forgot about that now. He was struck with how pretty she looked. That was something he hadn't predicted, that all cleaned up she'd be a pretty girl. Back when he saw her face for the first time at the waterfall, it was dirty, smeared with blood, and terrified. There was nothing pretty about it.

Mary yanked the sheet over her face.

"Sorry," Joe said.

He looked away, sort of flustered and confused all at once. Although when he turned his head to look at her again, she was peeking at him from above the sheet. She held it just below her eyes, which seemed to beam at him. He'd never seen eyes shine like that before. She must've been embarrassed because she ducked her head under the sheet once more.

"What do you think of that bed?" Joe asked. "I wasn't kidding when I said it would feel great, was I?"

"I've never slept in a bed," Mary replied.

She spoke through the sheet. A little pocket of fabric trembled from her breath. Joe thought for a moment about what she said. He knew she slept on the floor in Mom and Dad's room back home, but he reckoned she must've had a bed at one time.

"Where'd you sleep, then?"

"On the floor."

"Your whole life?"

"As long as I remember, I slept on the floor."

"And where was that?" he said. "Where you slept on the floor?"

"Down south."

"In the swamps, you mean? That far south?"

"No," Mary said. "The plains."

He knew it! She was from the plains, just like him.

"So you're from the southern plains."

"Near the swamps."

She still had the sheet pulled over her face, and it was sort of weird to talk to her like that. Her voice made the sheet quiver. But as long as she was talking, he didn't care.

"So what happened?"

She didn't answer now.

"You get raided or something? Diseases get you? What happened to your mom and dad? They get killed?"

She shook her head beneath the sheet.

"No?"

She shook her head again.

"They're not killed, you mean?"

"Stop," she said.

It finally sunk in that she didn't want to talk about it. He felt bad for peppering her with those questions, as if it was a game. And he wanted to cheer her up now, or at least take her mind off what he'd provoked.

"Well, now you got a big soft bed to sleep in. You can't beat that. And when I get that money, I'm going to get you some proper things. Whatever you want. What do you think of that?"

She didn't respond.

"Whatever you want," he said again. "I swear."

"I don't want any things," she said, still speaking through the sheet.

"You're just saying that. Everybody wants things."

"Not me."

"Not even a new dress?"

She didn't say anything at first.

"Maybe one," she said.

"Only one? I could buy you a dozen."

"Just one," she said again. "A red one."

"Red it is."

Joe sat on the bed. He pulled his feet up on the mattress and propped the pillow up behind his back. He glanced at Mary. The sheet inched down over her forehead, then over her light yellow eyebrows, and lower still over her closed eyelids. She kept inching the sheet down, past her little nose and her pale lips, until her whole face appeared. Her wet hair seemed to shine, and her skin seemed to glow like the first snow in winter.

When he was a kid and he saw the first snow gleaming in the morning sun, he desperately wanted to touch it. The smooth powder always proved irresistible. He'd run out the door before he was clothed properly while Mom shouted for him to put on his coat and boots. But some things couldn't wait.

As Joe stared at Mary, she opened her eyes. Her lashes fluttered before she looked up at him. He turned away, suddenly nervous, and ran his hands along his pants, although he didn't know why. He wondered if she could see what he was thinking and if all his feelings were transparent now. It made him feel vulnerable, and he didn't like it. When he looked at her again, her eyes were closed, and he felt more at ease then.

Joe heard a distant explosion outside. Next door, a woman screamed and something slammed against the wall. A siren blared. Mary curled into a caterpillar. He didn't feel so safe in the room anymore. For a moment Joe wished they were back at the waterfall, where everything seemed peaceful. He wished they could've stayed the night in the cave's cocoon and pretended they didn't have a care in the world.

He swung his legs out of bed, stood up, and walked to the dresser. He grabbed his recorder and brought it back to bed with him. Mary moved a little, but she didn't open her eyes. She was obviously tired. He twisted the two parts of the recorder together and licked the tip. Then he blew softly into the recorder and played "Blackbird" for her.

After she went to sleep, he lay awake. But instead of thinking about the feelings he was having for Mary, he worried. He wondered if the proprietor really told those ruffians to go away. And even if he had, the stable was still unlocked. Joe was worried about someone finding the diesel. He was also worried about the man in the kitchen who was suspicious of what he had in the wagon. He worried about getting caught or turned in for a reward. And then what would happen to them? He couldn't shut his mind off. It was irritating. He had to check the wagon again to make sure everything was okay, or else he'd never be able to fall asleep.

He got up, careful not to disturb Mary. He slipped out of the room, down the stairs, and out the back door. Even though it was only dusk, it seemed much later. All the buildings had a way of squeezing out the sky and making it seem darker. He walked to the stable. The ruffians were gone. He looked under the floorboards in the cab and was relieved to see the diesel still there. Nevertheless, he decided to spend the night in the wagon cab. He was still afraid someone was going to steal the diesel or turn them in for some kind of reward, and he couldn't let that happen now that they'd made it this far.

Although he knew he'd be leaving Mary alone, he also knew he always woke up at first light. He'd been that way as long as he could remember. He simply burst wide awake and leapt out of bed as if he couldn't waste another minute sleeping and needed to charge into the new day as if some great surprise awaited him. On their journey so far, he'd been up every morning before Mary even stirred. Matter of fact, he had to wake her most of the time and help her into the cab where she slept some more. That's what made him think he could get back to the room in the morning without her ever knowing he'd been gone.

Joe was more tired than he realized and before long he fell asleep. He'd only been asleep for an hour or so when a loud whirling sound shook him awake. The noise seemed to be coming right through the stable roof. He covered his head with his arms, expecting whatever it was to come crashing down on him. A bright light flashed through the stable windows and flooded the entrance. Joe thought maybe the young ruffians or the man in the kitchen had told the police about him. Either way, he was ready to make a run for it.

The whirling sound began to fade. The farther away it got, the safer Joe felt. When it was nearly silent, he realized the noise had probably been from a helicraft. He thought if he acted fast enough he could see it before it was completely gone. He ran outside, not even thinking if it was a good idea or not, and looked into the sky above the rooming house. Floating away into the dark was his first glimpse of a real helicraft. Although all he really saw was a dark object lit with bright lights.

That excitement soon vanished when he remembered Mary was all alone. No doubt she was awakened by the noise and was now panic-stricken to find him not there. He sprinted to the backdoor, flung it open, dashed through the kitchen, down the hall, and raced up the stairs, two at a time, until he reached the landing. The door was already open. He ran through the doorway and found a man in his underpants shaking a belt at Mary.

The man yelled, "Shut the hell up!"

He wielded the belt as if he was going to strike her.

"Stop!" Joe shouted.

The man turned. He was the same one from the kitchen, with the mouth ringed with whiskers.

"Oh, it's you again. Does this howling dog belong to you?"

"She belongs to me."

"Well, shut her up before I shut her up for you."

"It's okay," he said to Mary.

She held the white sheet up to her nose. Her eyes screamed, but she didn't make a sound. She withdrew her arm from behind the sheet and reached out to Joe.

The woman with the lumpy face and bruised eye appeared in the doorway.

"Did you give it to her?" she said. Her voice held a hint of glee.

"What did I tell you?" the man yelled. "Get back in that room."

He brushed by Joe and went into the hall. The woman cowered against the wall and looked up with a pleading face that soon went slack. When the man raised the belt above his head, she closed her eyes, not even cringing. Her face turned strangely serene. The man whipped the belt down across the woman's chest. She groaned and slumped to the floor while the man brought the belt above his head again to deliver another blow. Joe couldn't believe he was going to strike her a second time. Joe hadn't seen any reason for the first one, let alone a second. He dove at the man and grabbed his arm before he was able to bring the belt down on the woman. He hooked an arm around the man's burly neck and cinched his legs around his waist. The man hunched over, swung around, and slammed Joe against the wall. It knocked Joe loose and he dropped on the floor.

By that time a crowd had gathered in the hall. Joe saw the proprietor.

"This won't be tolerated!" he shouted.

Another man suddenly emerged. He had curly black hair all over his bare chest. He grabbed both Joe and the other man and dragged them outside into the dark street.

"You are evicted," the proprietor said. "Both of you."

Joe looked around for Mary. He didn't see her anywhere. He tried to run back into the rooming house, but the man with the bare chest pushed him to the ground.

"Hold it. Take your skinny ass somewhere else. You're not coming back in here. Do yourself a favor and don't make any more trouble."

"I have to get Mary."

Then Joe saw her peering out from behind the side of the house. He knocked the man's arm away and ran to her. He grabbed her hand and they scurried to the stable. He was surprised to find the horses already hitched and the wagon ready to go. He stared at Mary in disbelief.

Chapter 28

Joe wasn't sure where to go now. Through the dark, sour-smelling streets, the lopsided wagon bumped and scraped along the cobblestones. Even though they'd lost the money for the room, Joe was glad to be out. He prayed he could find another place so Mary could finally sleep in a real bed and he could make up for leaving her alone. In some ways, he felt torn. He had to protect the diesel, but he also had to protect Mary.

The tire rim clunked in a hole. It reminded Joe that he still needed to get a new tire. He didn't know why he hadn't asked the proprietor earlier if he knew where to get one. Joe guessed he forgot to ask because he got caught up in everything else that was going on. But he couldn't have lapses like that. He needed to stay on top of what was necessary. He couldn't be watching television and lose track of why they'd come here.

To the south, he saw tall buildings with checkerboard squares of yellow light and towers with more lights blinking red and blue. The area glowed like something white-hot was burning at the heart of it. All the light drenched the dark sky above with a bright dome. It appeared like a different world, like a dream world, a fantasy. Joe knew it was part of the forbidden Green Zone, and he had no business going there, yet he went anyway, hoping they'd get through and find a nice place to stay.

Joe turned down a dark alley toward the brightly lit buildings. Ahead of them was a gate with a Guardian Party symbol next to a small guardhouse. Maybe going this way wasn't such a good idea, he thought, especially after a light erupted in his face. He threw up his hands to ward it off. Squinting against the painful glare, he quickly turned the wagon around and trotted away.

Eventually they passed under a sign that read "Fulfillment District" in gleaming red letters. It led into a raucous street. What he witnessed looked like a festival at first, full of cheers and shouts and music, until he was in the thick of it. Then it was something much different. Drunken men stumbled about, shouting and laughing. Half-clothed women in doorways or on balconies jeered and whistled and flashed their bodies. Neon signs in blue and red and pink sizzled with names like Rodeo Girls, Cats a Go-Go, Sleazy Liz's, Cheap Sex, Packaged Liquor, and Beer! Beer! Beer! Other signs blinked: "Pleasure is Peace" and "Fulfillment is Freedom." More slogans to add to the others about security and sacrifice.

He'd never seen people so drunk like this, acting crazy and out-of-control as if it was all normal. He also couldn't believe how many people were jammed into the streets and rolling out of bars, brothels, and theaters. The swirling crowds had no sense of propriety. It stood in stark contrast to the way he had been raised. The

Prophet Roy Neolin preached, "Simplicity, humility, unity." He said the flesh should be denied in favor of the community. That's why Joe wore brown pants and a green shirt that covered all his skin except his head and hands. That's why women wore long dresses and high collars. Yet here were countless women parading bare legs, bare shoulders, and bare breasts. They all seemed perfectly happy with that, not a care in the world, not an ounce of shame. Joe didn't know whether to close his eyes to shut it out or keep them open so he didn't get sucked into it.

Without warning, a man with a bloody face spilled out of the darkness and reached inside the wagon cab at Joe. He managed to latch onto Joe's shirt and pull on it. The blood on his face flowed from a gash at the top of his forehead. He smiled as if Joe were an old friend. His eyes were at once glassy and wild. Then he tried to step into the wagon by using Joe to pull himself up. He jabbed a knee into the cab beneath Joe's legs, but Joe fended him off. He kicked the man's knee out and pried his hands loose from his shirt. He shoved the man back into the swollen crowd. After that, Joe wanted to rush through the rest of the street to get away, but the crush of people made it impossible. It was like slogging through thick mud.

At the end of the district, away from the noise and lights, Joe found another rooming house and stable. The house had a sagging veranda that wrapped around the front like a rotting old riverboat grounded in some shoals. No one was in the stable, only a few horses in stalls and a fancy wagon painted red. A decrepit motorbike in a far corner caught Joe's attention, although not enough for him to investigate. He had only one thing on his mind now. First thing tomorrow morning he was going to find the fat man that Frank had told him about, sell the diesel, and get them out of there. This was no place for a human being. Before he left the wagon in the stable, Joe shoved his handmade recorder in his back pocket.

At the door of the rooming house, he rapped the brass knocker and waited. The door cracked open and a thin line of faint light snuck out before a big eye appeared in the opening. The eye blinked. It blinked again. The door swung open. Standing there was a thin man with an abundance of white hair. It not only erupted from his eyebrows but also shot out his ears and poked out his head like twigs.

"For God's sake, don't just stand there, come in if you're coming in or get lost," he said. "Make up your damn mind."

After Joe led Mary inside, the hairy man let the door swing shut with a bang, and then he crouched in a chair in front of a small cabinet. He flipped a latch at the top and lowered a panel that rested above his knees as a desk. Inside were dozens of tiny drawers and holes stuffed with old papers that had turned yellow and brown. He pulled out a ledger and thumbed through the pages until he came to the page he was looking for. A buzzing sound started coming from the pocket on his vest.

"Confound it. Hold on. I got a call."

He tugged on a gold chain dangling from his vest pocket and pulled out a small tablet-like device with a glowing screen on it. Joe knew what it was immediately. It was definitely a mobicom. The landlord set it on the desk, tapped his ear a few times and suddenly a wavering image of a woman's face appeared hovering in the air above the mobicom. It startled Mary. She stepped back and scooted behind Joe. He knew she'd never seen anything like that before.

"It's nothing to be afraid of," he said. "It's just a picture."

"Hi, Margaret," the landlord said. His voice was surprisingly nice and friendly. "Can I call you back? I'm checking some folks in right now."

The wavering image of Margaret made a frowning face.

"So this isn't a good time?" she said.

"No, not exactly. I'm sorry, but I'll be free in minute like I said earlier today."

"Alright, alright. I can wait."

"Thank you, dear," the landlord said.

The image disappeared and the landlord grabbed the mobicom off the desk and stuffed it back in his vest pocket. Without missing a beat, he turned to Joe and Mary again and barked out, "It's by the week or month. No day rents, and no negotiations. You got that? You pay it all up front or you hit the bricks."

"We only need a room for a couple of days."

"What did I just say? A week or a month or nothing."

Joe didn't want to pay for a week, but he also didn't want go looking for another place to stay. He figured they would have plenty of money soon enough. He dug in his pocket and pulled out his drawstring purse and showed it to the landlord.

"That'll do." He snatched the purse out of Joe's hand and dumped all the money on the ledger.

"Hey," Joe said. "Wait. That's all we got."

Joe yanked the purse back and grabbed at the spilled coins, but the landlord swatted his hand away.

"Let me count it," the landlord said.

"Not all of it."

"It might be all of it."

"How much for a week?"

"Let me count it first."

"No. How much is it?"

Someone spoke over Joe's shoulder. It was a woman's voice. He didn't dare look to see who it was because he was afraid the landlord would grab the money when he wasn't looking.

"Twenty shekels," the woman said.

"Who asked you?" shouted the landlord. "Twenty-five for two."

The landlord scooped up the coins, but Joe grabbed his hand and peeled it open first. He looked at the coins and picked a piece out. Then he picked up the few coins left on the ledger. He dropped them in his purse and tightened the strings.

"Wrists," the landlord said.

Joe stuck his arm out and nudged Mary to do the same. As the landlord pulled out his mobicom again, Joe remembered about the tire.

"What do I look like, a junk yard?" the landlord said.

"You have to go to the Industrial District, near the lakeshore," came the woman's voice again.

This time Joe peered over his shoulder. He looked into a dusky side room. A dark-haired, dark-skinned woman sat sprawled on a shabby sofa. Beside her was a fireplace with orange flames in it. Her feet rested on a short table in front of her. White stockings were rolled down her dark legs and looped around her ankles. It was hard not to stare. Her arms were draped along the top of the sofa. In one hand she held a cigarette that she brought slowly to her mouth by bending only her elbow and turning her face, as if any more effort than that was too much. After she blew out a stream of smoke, she glanced at Joe through half-closed eyes.

Just then another woman appeared with her back to Joe. He turned a little more so he could see what was happening. The woman wore a shiny black slip that hugged her wide hips. She walked up to the dark-skinned woman on the couch and sat on the table in front of her. The dark-skinned woman leaned forward. With the flat of her hand she held her cigarette out to the lips of the other woman who took a drag.

"Don't smoke the whole thing, Ina," the dark-skinned woman said. "These aren't cheap."

Ina let go of the cigarette and coughed out smoke while she laughed and patted her chest.

"Sorry," she said. "It just felt so good."

"Put your eyes back in your head," said the landlord. "Those are dancing girls. Besides, you got your hands full anyway." Then he raised his voice. "Ava over there used to be something special, a mistress to a top official in the Ministry of Peace and Security. But she screwed that up. Isn't that right, sweetheart?"

"I can hear you, Walt," said Ava. She held the cigarette to her lips, breathed in, and then blew the smoke out in such a way that it fluttered in the air. "You don't have to shout, either. Give it a rest, why don't you?"

"I'm only trying to fill them in on our local celebrity."

"They don't need to know."

"You're just jealous," Ina said to the landlord, "because you want a piece of that too."

"Shut up, fat ass," the landlord said.

"Fat ass? Fat ass?" Ina said. "You only wish you could get some of this fat ass." She leaned to her side, lifted her thigh, and grabbed a hunk of her bottom and shook it.

"Strumpets," the landlord said, derisively.

"Speak up, you old wart," Ina said. "We can't hear you."

The landlord didn't say anything after that. He slapped the key down on the desktop and mumbled, "Room 13. Up the stairs and to your right."

When Joe reached for the key, the landlord kept his hand over it. The landlord was obviously the kind of person that enjoyed making other people feel small, and as much as Joe wanted to pound his fist on the landlord's hand to get him to let go of the key, he resisted. He realized this wasn't a big deal and not worth making a scene over. Little by little he was getting smarter. "Choose your battles." It was something Frank always said that Joe didn't pay any attention to because he thought everything was worth a fight. He was beginning to realize what Frank meant. Not until Joe withdrew his hand did the landlord uncover the key.

Chapter 29

Joe and Mary turned in front of the doorway into the room where the two women sat. The strap on Ina's slip had fallen off her shoulder and she rolled it back up with the palm of her hand.

When she saw them, she said, "Oh my. That tiny little thing is pregnant. She's about to burst."

Joe didn't know what to say, or if he was supposed to say anything, although he didn't like the way she seemed so surprised at Mary's condition, like there was something defective about her being pregnant. He wanted to defend Mary and say there wasn't a single defective thing about her. It was none of Ina's business anyway. But he held his tongue. The last thing he wanted to do was blow their cover.

Ava glanced at Joe and then flicked her spent cigarette in the fireplace. She tapped another one out from a silver case and struck a match against it to light her new one.

Joe knew he should've just gone up to their room and forgotten about the women, especially since the two "strumpets" seemed to have already forgotten about them, but he couldn't. He'd never talked to such women before. Until an hour ago he never knew such women existed. Sure, the old hermit Hans talked of "ladies of the night" and traders spoke of "good-time girls," but Joe never imagined them being this brazen and nonchalant about how they looked and how they acted. Besides, Frank never said anything about "dancing girls" or "strumpets" or even the Fulfillment District. Maybe he left that part out, or maybe they'd gotten way off course in the city.

Suddenly Ina noticed them again, as if they'd snuck up on her somehow.

"Did you want to say something, honey?" she said.

He'd been repressing himself so hard that he finally let go.

"She's my girl," he blurted out. "She's breech. We're here to go to the hospital. Give birth. Our folks died of PB. We're all we got. That's it. That's our story."

"Slow down, dear," Ina said. "We're not interrogating you."

Ava looked at him for a lingering moment, as if she were trying to figure him out, before she said something that alarmed Joe.

"Who told you to say that?"

"No one," he said quickly. "That's the truth."

"Well, it didn't sound like the truth. It sounded like you were repeating what somebody told you. You need to learn how to lie better."

"Leave him alone," Ina said. "They're just a couple of dirt-eaters. He's probably scared. Never been to the city before."

"Being a good liar is the only way to survive," Ava continued. "And if he doesn't want to find himself in a labor prison or his girl's baby given to some fat cats in the Green Zone, then he better learn to lie better."

"Don't be so hard."

"I'm only trying to help. How is that being hard?"

"I'm just saying you see the bad in everything and you aren't open to anything else."

"No, I see reality. I see things for what they are."

Ina shook her head.

"Give me another drag on that," she said, and reached out for Ava's cigarette. She took a smoke and handed it back to Ava.

"They're still looking at us," Ava said, "like we're the weird ones."

They both laughed.

"It's okay, sugar," Ina said. "You go on up to your room."

"You going to tuck them in too?" Ava asked.

"Maybe I will."

"Mama's going to make them feel good."

"Now why do you have to say something like that?"

"Mama gives good love."

"You are nasty. You have to dirty up anything innocent, don't you?"

"That's the truth."

"You can't stand anything nice."

"Only if it's nice for me."

"Where's your heart?"

"In the same place as the truth."

They both laughed again.

Ava said, "They're still looking at us."

"Shoo, now," Ina said. "Or Mama won't bring you milk and cookies."

They laughed yet again, but Joe didn't get the joke, or any of the jokes they were laughing about. It seemed like they were speaking a different language. And he didn't like that. Maybe nothing was making sense on account of how exhausted he felt. Maybe his mind was all hazy from stress and fatigue. All the same, he got the distinct feeling they were making fun of him. He felt foolish now for being drawn in by these women and standing there, just like a typical bumpkiny dirt-eater, listening to them prattle on about nonsense. He only wanted to rest now, to let the day fade away, and to wake up to a new day that felt better for both of them. They didn't belong here, that was for sure.

Chapter 30

Inside the room, Mary immediately crawled onto the bed. She turned on her side and brought her knees up against her big belly and tucked her head in against her breast.

"From here on out," Joe said, "I think everything is going to be fine. There's just one thing left to do and that won't be hard because Frank told me who to talk to. We just have to say we know Frank, and the rest should be easy. I know we're in a crazy place and none of it makes any sense to you, but we'll be gone soon. We'll be back home before you know it."

Mary didn't move a muscle. She stayed curled up like a hard little ball. Then her body flinched with a spasm, and she wriggled her hips as if in discomfort.

"You okay?" Joe said. "Was it the baby? Is it moving, kicking?"

He didn't like how she was all balled up and non-responsive, like a scared centipede. He was afraid she was reverting back to her old self. If she went back there, she might not ever come out again.

He had to help her somehow, but he didn't have a clue as to what to do. Maybe she was hungry. She had to be. They hadn't eaten since they got to the city. Maybe the baby inside was hungry and upset about it. Maybe she'd feel better if she got some food. They had half a jar of vegetable chowder and some pinole left in the wagon.

"I'm going to get some food out of the wagon," he said. He pulled the recorder out of his back pocket and set it on the table. "Once you eat something, your spirits will lift. I'll be right back."

He hated to leave her, but he didn't have any choice.

Downstairs he saw Ava still sitting on the couch. She had her head back as she stared at the ceiling. She wasn't smoking anymore. The flames in the fireplace had died down. Joe didn't know if he should say hello. He thought he should at least be friendly since she talked to him earlier, even though she wasn't particularly nice after that. But she didn't seem to notice him and he didn't want to disturb her, so he continued on to the front door. Besides, he was more interested in getting food for Mary.

"Where are you sneaking off to?"

Joe stopped and turned. It was Ava.

"I'm going out to our wagon."

"For what?"

"I forgot something."

"You don't know what it is?" she said.

"Just something I forgot."

"So you can't tell me?"

"If I did I wouldn't be following what you said earlier."

She smiled. "About lying, you mean."

"Yes."

"That wasn't lying."

"What was it, then?

"Hiding, which only makes you look suspicious."

"So I should've said I was going to get my recorder."

"Only if that's a lie."

"If I said yes, it wouldn't be a lie anymore."

"You're catching on."

Ava leaned her head back again and looked at the ceiling. Joe was about to leave when he couldn't resist asking her something.

"What were you thinking before?" he said.

"Before what?"

"Before you called out to me. I saw you looking up like you were thinking."

"It's best to stay out of other people's business unless you want something from them."

"I was only being friendly. That's all I wanted."

"Don't make that mistake again."

She turned away and grabbed the poker beside the couch and stoked the flames. Joe couldn't figure her out. One minute it seemed like she might be nice, then the next minute she seemed mean and cold.

He left her alone. Why was he even bothering with her, anyway, when his chief concern was Mary?

He unlocked the front door and walked outside onto the porch. The night smelled like it was burning, like burning ash in a fire pit. The darkness was thick and hazy. He heard the clomp-clomp of hooves and the squeak of wheels as a horse and wagon drove past.

When he reached the stable, he lifted the wood latch, peeled open one panel of the double doors, and slipped inside the darkness. He felt for the lantern he saw earlier hanging from a nail beside the door. Then he fumbled for a wood match from a tin can hanging from another nail. He set the lantern on the ground, pumped the valve, and lit the mantle.

At the wagon, he lifted the lantern over the side of the bed and peered in, but all he saw were crumpled blankets. He panicked. He set the lantern down in the bed and scrambled over the side. He grabbed the blankets and flung them out of the way. There was nothing beneath. All the water, the pinole, and the half jar of vegetable chowder were gone. All of it. Joe snatched the lantern and jumped out of the bed. Inside the cab, he tore up the floorboards, expecting the worst. When he saw that the bundled-up diesel was still there, he breathed a little easier.

Back inside the rooming house, Ava was gone, but the hairy landlord was standing there with a scowl on his face.

"This place is locked up for the night. There's a blackout coming." He paused and rummaged in his vest pocket and pulled out his mobicom.

"But I only went out once," Joe said.

"Don't get smart with me."

"Is there any food we can have?"

"What's with all the questions? You only paid for a room."

"How much is food?"

"How much do you have left?"

"Just give me a price," Joe said.

"Twenty-five."

"I don't have that."

"Not my problem."

"What if I just buy a little bit, enough for tonight?"

"Room and board for a week is fifty, no exceptions. This isn't a charity."

"But my girl is hungry."

"Open your ears. Not my problem. Either pay up or scram."

"How do we get food, then?"

"Like all the rest of the mooches and riffraff."

"Where's that?"

"Figure it out for yourself!"

"Why are you being this way?" Joe fumed. "Would it kill you to help us? Forget it."

Joe stomped up the stairs and down the hall to their room. He inserted the key, pushed the door open, and locked it behind him. Mary was still curled up on the bed. He hoped she was asleep and not waiting for something to eat. When he sat on the bed, she stretched out and pushed herself up on her elbows. He was glad to see that because it meant she wasn't retreating back into her shell, but it also meant she was probably expecting some food.

"Our stuff was stolen," he said. "So we don't have anything to eat. I'm sorry. It's my fault. We should've brought it in with us, so we would have it. And that stupid landlord won't help us."

Mary didn't make a move at first. Then she sunk back into the bed. She drew her legs up against her belly as tight as she could and curved the rest of her body around her stomach and huddled close beside him. Joe couldn't stand to see her disappointed.

"I can go out tonight and find some. I won't be long."

"No," she said. "Stay here."

"Honest, I won't be long. I know just where to go," he lied.

"Please," she said, "stay."

"Okay. If that's what you want."

"Play for me," she said.

Joe stood up. The bed creaked as the mattress rose, rocking Mary's coiled body. Joe walked to the dresser, picked up his recorder, and returned to the bed. Before they left on their journey, he never imagined how important his recorder would be. He'd brought it for his own pleasure, never thinking he could share that pleasure with Mary too.

He got out his recorder and played it quietly, like a whisper, next to her ear. He sang the lullaby that he told her was just for her.

> "Sleep my child and stars attend thee,
> All through the night . . .
> I my loved ones' vigil keeping,
> All through the night."

But before he could finish singing, there was a soft snapping sound, and then all the lights went out.

Chapter 31

The next morning, in Joe's haste to sell the diesel and get out of the city as fast as possible, he convinced himself to forego getting any food until after the sale. He didn't think it would take much time. He considered what was worse, being a little hungry or staying in the city any longer than they had to? Aside from that, Mary slept through the whole night and seemed to be in better spirits that morning. He thought everything was okay for now.

He took her along to search for the Industrial District and to find the steel mill where Frank had worked. It was where his older brother had told him he could find a buyer for the diesel. "Look for the fat man," Frank had said. "His name's Templeton." Frank knew because he had spent six months shoveling ore, limestone, and coke for a blast furnace. That was until he severed three fingers in a slag wagon that might've killed him if not for the heroics of the fat man named Templeton. When

Frank returned to the farm, he was plagued with nightmares about living in the city. He said he'd never go back, but he had a pocketful of money that kept the family going. While he was there, he learned about the black market in illegal fuel. It was a dangerous game. The consequences were violent death. "Take whatever he'll give you and get out of there," Frank said.

Eventually they reached the shore of Lake Mashenomak, which really wasn't a shore at all, but a concrete cliff. It dropped down to black waves tipped with white flecks of spume that lapped against the foam along the wall below. Joe stood on the edge with Mary and looked out across the black lake to a long string of windmills stretching in both directions, and then he looked even farther to where the lake disappeared over the horizon. The amount of water, the sheer size of Lake Mashenomak, was incredible to Joe. The most water he had ever seen at one time was at the waterfall. Other than that he knew water only in terms of rivers and streams. How far did the lake go? How deep did it get? What could possibly be on the other side? Who lived there?

What was even better was to finally see the clear blue sky spreading out over the water. Seeing it reminded Joe of home and how long it had been since he'd seen an unadulterated sky. In the city, all the buildings and lights seemed to cram out the sky, so you didn't even notice it. It was something far in the background and not something that wrapped around you at every moment.

Back home, he was always aware of the sky, especially at night. He wondered how people survived without seeing the stars and the moon. Joe couldn't imagine how, but obviously people did. One of his favorite things was to lie on his back in the pasture and look up at all the stars in the night. Gazing at the stars always filled him with a sense of wonder, both big and small. He felt part of something greater than just himself—after all, somewhere up there was the paradise of Welkenglebe, where Virid lived—but at the same time, all that greatness made him feel small. Yet somehow he didn't feel insignificant. Far from it. He felt like he expanded, like he grew larger because those millions of stars glowing out there in the endless dark were also a part of him too.

"Back home the sky is endless," Joe mused. "But the land is small. While here the sky is small, but the city seems endless. You know what I mean? I guess what I'm trying to say is I prefer lots of sky."

"Me too," Mary said.

"We're sky people, you and me. We're people who need skies. Day skies, night skies. Skies all the time. Frank would say that's a bunch of nonsense, but that's what I think. You can't help how you think, right?"

"Right. We're sky people."

"Absolutely. Hey, when we get back home, we can lie out under the stars together. Just stretch out, side by side, and stare at all the stars. I love doing that. You can even pick a star out to be your very own, and then whenever you look into the night you will see your star. It will be your star forever. I'll pick one too. We can both have stars. And the baby. What do you say to that?"

Mary didn't reply, so Joe thought maybe she figured he was foolish. But that couldn't be true. She agreed with him about being "sky people." So maybe she was only longing for home like him.

In the distance to his right was a platform standing above the water with blinking lights on its towers. And along a pier sat an idling ship with huge smokestacks. Up and down the wharf, carts and wagons and men bustled about. Small motorized trucks emblazoned with the Guardian symbol puttered and zipped among the traffic under the shadow of countless more towers and smokestacks. Joe drove the wagon in that direction. It limped as the tire rim scraped on the ground.

They passed a huge white cooling tower for a nuclear reactor. White steam rose out the top. They rode across a bridge spanning a viaduct of streaming water that flowed out into the lake where a cloud of fog churned. Further on, they went by a long row of green algae tubes nearly a hundred meters tall. Behind them were solar collectors to fuel lights in the center of the tubes in order to keep heating the algae during the night. Before long they came to a fenced lot with a heaping mound of black tires within it. Joe stopped in front of a small office that looked more like a shanty. Inside, a young man greeted Joe with a hearty hello. He had a bulging cheek and wore a dented derby hat with a frayed brim.

"What brings you here?" The bulge in his cheek moved.

"I need a tire," Joe said.

"You don't say. What a coincidence. I'm up to my ass in tires." He smiled, showing teeth coated in something like brown shellac. He spit a thick jet of brown saliva that splatted into a tin bucket.

"Let's take a look-see at your situation."

Outside, the young man inspected the rim and kicked and squeezed the other tires.

"What you need is all four replaced. But I can see you aren't a man of means. What kind of means do you have?"

"I don't know what you mean," Joe said.

The young man laughed. "That's funny. I'm talking money here."

"I don't have much." Then Joe wished he hadn't said that.

"That's not good. How much do you have?"

"How much are the tires?"

"For all four?"

"For one."

"You're going to need two at least."

"Okay. Two."

"Forty shekels."

Joe knew he didn't have that, but he didn't want the young man to know. Then he remembered what was in his pocket. "I got rifle shells."

"Rifle shells? No kidding? Let me see them."

Joe fished the five shells he had left out of his pocket and showed them to the young man.

"That's serious."

"How about ten shekels and two shells?"

The young man thought a moment. He spit a brown wad on the ground. "That sounds fair enough."

Half an hour later they were running smoothly on a new tire with a spare sitting in the back. Even though he was down to three bullets, he was glad he didn't have to give up his recorder or pocketknife. If it came down to it, he would've given up his pocketknife before the recorder, although the pocketknife would've certainly been more useful. But the more Joe thought about it, the more he realized those extra bullets would've been valuable for hunting and protection on their way back home. That is if they even made it out of the city alive to get home in the first place.

Chapter 32

They passed an area that had giant boilers attached to a series of tubes. Spiky towers shot blue and orange flames into the sky. Beyond that, not far from the idling ship, he steered the wagon down a dark cinder-covered path. The path ran between a line of railroad cars full of coal and the grimy black walls of the steel mill. Up ahead, bursts of red and orange light shot out of a doorway like gun blasts. And up above, through the open slits of darkened windows, more bursts of orange and red light.

This was the place where Frank lost his fingers, where flying sparks singed his clothes and burned scars onto his skin, where the heat made him sweat in torrents and made his muscles ache at the end of the day, where the smoke clogged his lungs and made him spit black globs like being caught in a choking dust storm. This was the place that Frank never wanted to go back to.

"You stay here," Joe said to Mary. "If you see anybody, duck down. If that doesn't work, tell them you're waiting for your dad inside the mill, okay?

"Okay," she said.

"I won't be long. I promise. We'll be headed home tonight. Don't worry."

Although Frank had told Joe about the steel mill, nothing really prepared him for seeing the real thing. The noise inside was thunderous. A clash of lights and spraying sparks. Massive steel beams, catwalks, dangling chains, and enormous swinging hooks. Buckets bubbled over, dripping with fiery red liquid. Filthy half-clothed men clung to it all like glowing ants. In the middle of all the chaos was a giant round blast furnace that was as big as a barn. It blazed with bright orange and yellow light. At the top, bare-chested men, shining with greasy sweat, heaved wagons of raw ingredients into the smoldering charge hole. Near the bottom, snakes of molten iron flowed like lava out of holes and into buckets, which were hoisted by chains as big as a man's leg and then poured into the volcanic top of another furnace.

At first, Joe was too overwhelmed to move. No wonder Frank had nightmares. He took a deep breath and looked around for the fat man, but he didn't see anyone who appeared to be particularly fat. Then he spotted a large muscular man wearing black bib overalls. He didn't wear a shirt underneath. His greasy skin glistened from the flashes of light. Strapped around his head were strange goggles that completely encased his eyes with two cones. He looked more like a creature than a man.

Joe felt as if he were walking up to a giant. When he stood next to the side of the goggled man, he noticed little cinder burns and scars all up and down his slick arm. Joe hesitated before he reached out and tugged on the overalls at the man's hip. He didn't know what to expect, so he braced himself. The man lifted his head as if catching a scent on the breeze. He looked over his shoulder and then down. The lenses in his goggles blazed with bursting red light before they turned black and Joe saw himself shrunken small in the dark lenses.

"I'm looking for the fat man," Joe said. "Templeton. He's a friend of Frank's. You know Frank?"

"Who the hell is Frank?"

"He's my brother. He worked here."

"Frank?" The man repeated it as if maybe he remembered. "And just who are you?"

He lifted the goggles off his eyes and pushed them up on his forehead where they looked like two horns sticking out.

"I told you. I'm Frank's brother. We're from the plains."

"Plains? You're a dirt-eater, then. Oh, hey, I remember him. Dirt-eater Frank. A real moron. Bitched and moaned."

That didn't sound like Frank to Joe. Sure, Frank could be gruff and ill-tempered, but rarely did he ever bitch and moan. His brother wasn't a complainer. He did what needed to be done with little fuss.

"That must be a different Frank."

"Oh, it's him, all right. Lost three fingers. That was funny as hell. Boy, did he wail. Blood shooting all over the place."

"That's not funny."

"You should've been there. It was funny."

"He's my brother."

"That doesn't say much for you."

"Frank's the best—"

But Joe didn't get a chance to finish because the man started shouting for someone else.

"Hey, Petey!" he shouted. "Come here. You got to see this."

A shirtless man, standing near a casting mold that glowed with yellow liquid, turned and waved his arm. His bare skin was slathered in greasy soot. He wore black gloves up to his elbows, which he tore off and slapped on the ground. Joe didn't know why Petey had to come see him. Maybe he knew where the fat man was and he could point Joe in the right direction. Maybe Petey was a friend of Frank's and that's why he'd been called over.

When Petey walked toward them, he moved like a hunk of rock on stiff pegs.

"What is it, Stan?" Petey said.

"Remember that dumbshit dirt-eater from a year ago?" Stan said. "Frank or something. The one who got his fingers caught on that slag wagon? Remember? We took him to get drunk one time and he screwed that strumpet and didn't even know it the next day."

"Oh, yeah," Petey said. "Kept saying when he got enough money he was going to leave this rotten place and go back home. Every damn day he said that. Annoying as hell. But he was fun to get all riled up."

"Yeah, that's him. Well, this here is his brother."

"No kidding? This little runt?"

"I'm not a runt," Joe said.

"Beg your pardon," Petey said.

"I'm looking for Templeton. He's a friend of Frank's."

"A friend?"

"You're dumber than your brother," Petey said.

"All that inbreeding," Stan added.

"Say what you want," Joe said. "I don't care."

"He's got the same spunk as his brother," Stan said. "That's for sure."

Joe was undeterred. "I got something for him."

"For Templeton?" Stan asked. "What?"

"It's only for him."

"I already told you he's gone today."

"If you tell me where he's at, I can go meet him."

"How should I know where that fat bastard lives?"

"I really need to find him. Does anybody know?"

"Open your ears, shit for brains."

"No," Joe said. "You open your ears. I asked does anybody else know, not if you still did. It's a different question, shit for brains."

Petey laughed. "He's got you there."

"Shut up," Stan said.

What Joe did next was a big risk. Frank told him to only talk to Templeton. No one else. Anybody different might turn Joe in for a reward. But he wanted to sell the diesel so desperately. He just wanted to get the money and go home.

"If you can't help me with Templeton, maybe you can help me yourself."

Stan's eyes rolled with exasperation. "You're a persistent little runt."

"It's important."

"What do you want, then?"

"It's a secret."

"Everything's a secret here. What makes yours so special?"

"It's in my wagon. The secret."

"Don't play games with me. You're on thin ice already."

Petey chimed in. "Let's take a look. It might be good for a laugh. What can it hurt?"

"Fine," Stan said. "Show us what it is."

After Joe stepped outside, the booming sound from inside the mill faded to a hum. But his ears were now ringing. He noticed Lester and Sam lifting their hooves like they were antsy. Joe looked around to see if there was any trouble. Then he felt a slight tremor in the ground, a vibration that must've been coming from the rumbling inside the steel mill, which was probably shivering up Lester and Sam's legs in a painful way. He saw Mary in the cab, just her hat sticking up above the dash. He hoped he hadn't made a mistake.

When they got to the side of the cab and the men could see Mary plainly, Stan said, "You got to be kidding me. No way." He waved his hand in front of him as if he were swatting away flies.

Joe was puzzled. "You don't know what it is yet."

"I can see what it is," Stan said. "And I'm not helping that fat pig find little girls. She's pregnant, for God's sake."

Joe looked at Mary again.

"No way," Stan said. "I'm not going to be any part of it."

"She hasn't got anything to do with this. I haven't even shown you what it is yet."

Petey laughed. "What is she, your sister?"

"I don't want to see her!" Stan shouted. "It's sick. You people are sick. Selling your pregnant sister off."

"No," Joe said. "She's not my sister. It's not her. Listen to me."

"No, you listen to me. Forget it."

"Just tell me where Templeton is at."

"I'm not telling you a thing." Stan bent down and stared into Joe's eyes. His breath smelled sour. "You're lucky I don't kill you. Take that girl back to her parents, now."

He turned and walked away. Petey shook his head and chuckled before he turned and followed Stan.

"Hey!" Joe shouted. "Hey!"

The men ignored him and disappeared inside the rumbling steel mill. Joe was so frustrated that he kicked the ground hard enough to send up a shower of black cinders.

"I got to go back in," Joe said to Mary. "Somebody in there has to know where Templeton is at."

That was as far as he got because up ahead around the corner came some kind of motorized cart. At least it looked like a cart. On top of its roof was a single whirling red light. Joe thought it was the police, so he jumped in the cab and shook the reins to get Lester and Sam going. After only a couple of steps, the cart was right alongside them. It didn't make any noise like a combustion engine, so it was probably electric. The man stepped out of the seat. He didn't look like a policeman; he didn't even have a helmet on, and his uniform had a strange insignia on it that Joe didn't recognize.

"What are you doing here?" he demanded.

"Nothing," Joe said.

"What do you mean nothing? You don't end up here by doing nothing."

"We took a wrong turn."

"This is private property, belongs to Spire-Samson Steel. And I'll need you to leave unless you have a permission tag."

"No, sir. Like I said, we took a wrong turn."

He took out a small scanner and held it toward Joe.

"I'll say you took a wrong turn," he said. "This ain't no hospital. Get going."

Joe flicked the reins and Lester and Sam plodded forward. The wagon lurched and squeaked on the rusty axle. After they'd gone a little ways, Joe looked back through the window. The security guard got in his cart, turned it around, and sped up close behind them. He was talking into his scanner now as he followed them all the way to the end of the steel mill, where he stopped. He sat there watching them as they rolled away. The little red light on top kept swirling.

After it was clear they were out of trouble, Joe realized this wasn't going to be so easy after all.

Off to the right, near the lakeshore, two towers shot flames of orange fire high into the air. He looked at Mary.

"I guess we'll have to come back tomorrow."

Mary coughed lightly, but Joe didn't pay much attention. He was too busy dwelling on their situation. They only had two days left now until their tags ran out. Then Mary coughed louder with a dry raspy sound to it.

"You okay?" Joe asked. "That didn't sound good. You're not getting sick, are you?"

"I'm okay," she said.

"It must be the air. It's not like the good air back home."

She coughed yet again.

"Breathe into your sleeve," Joe said.

She brought the crook of her arm against her mouth.

"We need to get you some food," Joe said. "I said I was going to last night but I didn't do it." He felt terrible now. He wished he'd done that first thing in the morning. Why hadn't he done it? What was he thinking? "You're probably getting weak, and if you get some food you'll be better."

Joe drove on beneath the dark buildings and the smokestacks spewing white and black smoke clouds. In the distance atop a thin tower was a white light like a star. But of course it wasn't a star, and seeing it didn't make Joe feel a sense of wonder. It made him feel trapped and small.

"We'll get you something to eat, Mary. Don't worry."

Chapter 33

Back at the rooming house, Joe held Mary's elbow and guided her up the creaky stairs. He couldn't believe how quickly she'd deteriorated. Her tiny elbow felt like a grainy knot of gristle between his thumb and fingers. He'd gotten used to how thin she was, so he didn't really notice if she was getting thinner. As he touched her now, with his palm against the sharp ridges of her spine, he wondered if their meager diet over the course of their journey was taking its toll on her, especially the last few days. After all, her body wasn't only responsible for sustaining itself; it was also responsible for the baby staying happy and growing inside her. The last decent meal they'd had was the fish at the waterfall.

Inside the room, Joe led Mary to the side of the bed where she sat down. He got on his knees and unlaced the frayed strings on her shoes and slid the tattered leather husks off her feet. Her toenails were dirty and her toes chafed red. The only thing he could do was make her comfortable until he got some food in her. He plumped a pillow up for her to prop her head against and he eased her hat off her head.

"I'll turn the television on," he said.

After the first night, she started to watch the television. She liked the moving pictures, as long as there was nothing scary about them. But she didn't like the sound, so he turned the volume down until it was silent.

A woman on the screen was twirling down the steps of a grand staircase in a dress that ruffled and floated around her legs.

Joe grabbed a chair from the table by the window. The legs scraped across the wood floor as he dragged it beside the bed. He sat down but couldn't stay still. He looked at Mary and then looked at the television screen. He clasped and unclasped his hands. He threaded his fingers together. He pressed his palms tight and twisted them like he was trying to unscrew the lid off a jar.

Finally, he had to do something. He was about to go out of his skin. She wasn't going to get better while he watched over her like a hen. He had no other choice than to go and search for food, no matter how long that took and what it cost. If he had to spend the last of their money and the rifle shells, he would have to do it. What was the alternative? He could steal, but what if he got caught? He could beg, but he had too much pride for that. Or he could ask Ava, but once again he wasn't one to ask for help if he thought he could do it on his own. Besides, tomorrow they would find Templeton and sell the diesel. Everything would be fine. They only needed enough food to make it through the rest of the day and night. That was all that mattered at the moment.

"I can make it," Mary said.

"I can't take that chance."

"We'll be going home tomorrow."

"I know that, but you need your strength now."

"I'm not what's important."

"What are you talking about? That's complete nonsense."

"The money's important."

"The money doesn't mean a thing if you're not okay."

"But I don't want you to go. I can make it."

She sat up and acted like she was going to crawl out of bed. But Joe grabbed her by the shoulders and stopped her.

"Let go," she said.

"No, you need to stay right here and rest."

"I'm fine."

"Mary, I'm serious."

"But if I'm fine, you won't have to go."

She twisted her shoulders to shake loose from his grip. "Now stop."

"No."

"Don't be so stubborn."

She surprised Joe by knocking his arms away. She was stronger than she looked. Then she swept her legs off the bed and sprang to her feet. She took two steps and turned to face him as if to prove there was nothing wrong with her. But there was definitely something wrong. She wavered a moment. Her already white face turned ghostly. Her eyelids trembled. She seemed to realize she was becoming faint and what that meant.

"I'm fine," she said. "You don't have to go."

Joe stood up because he thought she was going to fall, but somehow she held herself steady.

"It's okay," Joe said. "Just listen to me. Sit down. You aren't well."

Joe inched toward her. He was afraid to grab her again because she might try to wrench free once more and really fall. When she coughed, her little shoulders jerked up and her chest sunk like a popped bubble. Her head drooped low and her hair hung down so he couldn't see her face at all. It was the way he was used to always seeing her.

"Come on, lay down," Joe said.

She didn't move. Joe stepped toward her, but before he could put his arms around her, she tilted forward and rested the crown of her head against his chest. He slid his arms along the sides of her hard belly and around her waist. Then he shifted her toward the bed again. She moved like a bundle of empty sacks in his arms. He set her on the bed gently before he bent down to lift her feet onto the sheets.

After he sat in the chair, she asked him, "What if you don't come back?"

"That's not going to happen," Joe said.

"How do you know?"

"I just know. You have to trust me."

He hoped she would confirm what he said by saying she did trust him or she did believe him, but she didn't open her mouth or look at him. Instead, she stared at the images flashing on the television. So this was how it was going to be, Joe thought. She was hardening herself for the worst, cocooning herself again in case he didn't return. No amount of talking was going to change that. It was the price he had to pay to make sure she was healthy again. She would understand, eventually.

Chapter 34

Downstairs, he opened the door and made sure not to lock it when he closed it. He even opened it again to be certain. Hopefully, when he got back, it would still be unlocked. If not, he could climb up on the side roof below their window and get back in the room that way.

Out in the street, he stood next to a hole in the uneven cobblestones. It was half full of muddy water. Across the street a few people sat on their stoops. There was a sulfuric smell in the air. A woman held a handkerchief to her mouth. A few pickup wagons rolled past and a car buggy pulled by two horses.

Joe kept to the side of the street as he walked toward the Fulfillment District. If there was any food to be had, it had to be there. Ahead of him, the bright lights blinked blue and red and yellow. They could almost be beautiful, if not for the fact that they were luring people in like flies.

Soon enough he was back along those seedy streets. He pushed through the crowd, barely able to stomach the stench of rotten sweat and sour vomit. He held his breath and endured the shoves and curses from the men he bumped into. As he passed the patio of a brothel, a strumpet painted like a clown spotted him and cooed to the others: "There's a young one, girls. Mmmm, ripe and fresh. Come here, boy. I'll take you for free." They laughed and called to him. One of them reached out and grabbed Joe by the arm. She yanked him against her body and shoved his face in her powdered bosom. He managed to tear himself away and tumbled into a crowd that erupted into hoots of laughter.

When he recovered himself, he peeked inside the door of a noisy bar. On a stage, a three-piece band played as topless women flounced and danced around in skirts. The rest of the big room was filled with tables of both men and women who were all drinking, smoking, and shouting. The air was clouded with white smoke.

A few doors down, he stepped inside a place that didn't seem as rowdy as the others. Matter of fact, it was fairly quiet. It was the Braun Theater. People sat around tables laden with empty dinner plates and leftover food. That was a good sign, no doubt. The crowd, however, was looking off to the right, so Joe craned his neck around a pillar to see what everyone was staring at.

On a stage was a scene set in a forest with ribbons of fire in the center. On a platform stood a priest wearing a feathered headdress and a snake around his neck. Off to the side were bare-chested men beating on drums. Scattered about the stage were fallen girls who were completely nude and covered in blood. Standing above them were even more nude girls, only they had daggers in their hands. At first, Joe was horrified because he thought they really stabbed them, but then he realized they were only pretending. It was a show, and the blood was fake, not real.

A voice behind Joe made him jump.

"You like the show?"

Joe felt embarrassed. He wanted to get out of there quickly, especially since he knew he was wasting time in finding food for Mary.

"Pardon me," the man said. "I didn't mean to scare you."

"You didn't scare me."

Joe was about to slip out of the theater and keep searching for someplace that might be selling food when he got a good look at the man. He was taken aback by what he saw. The man looked almost exactly like the man in the fedora hat that he saw on television. He had the same half-smirk, half-grin on his face, and the same brown eyes that shimmered like he knew a secret you wanted to know.

"I can see you're not from around here," the man said.

"Don't call me a dirt-eater," Joe said.

"I won't. My name's Phil, by the way. My great grandfather was a plainsman." *Plainsman*, Joe liked the sound of that. "But he left shortly after the power grids went down out there and they first outlawed oil."

"That was a long time ago."

Phil chuckled. "Yes. Things have changed since then. Gotten worse, I hear. Is that why you're here? Your family has moved to the city?"

"No," Joe said.

Phil adjusted his hat, shifted his weight a little, and balled his fists in the pockets of his jacket. Inside his lapels he wore a red tie knotted at his neck.

"I'm here because my girl is breech," Joe said. He remembered to stick to his story. "When she gives birth, we're going back. She's really hungry. I need to find some food. Do you know where I can get some?"

"Certainly, I'll buy you whatever you want."

Joe almost said yes right away because the offer was too tempting and he wouldn't have to spend any money or rifle shells. The problem was he had a queer feeling about this guy. Even so, he thought he'd be a fool not to at least follow the guy to where there was some food. He would just have to be careful. That's all. At the first sign of trouble, he'd simply run.

"I can pay for it, just show me where to go."

"A man of pride, I see."

Joe followed Phil down a side street off the crowded Fulfillment District. Moments later, they entered some kind of market with stalls and storefronts that lined the street of medium-sized buildings. It smelled of ripe sweat and fried meat. On top of some of the buildings were heliports where government officials and the wealthy docked their helicrafts.

The market below bustled with all sorts of different people. Men and women shouted and gestured at each other as if they were trying to outdo one another. Some were dressed in rags, scuttling about or scavenging for anything dropped or discarded. A woman, who had a flattened nose that looked punched in, snatched an apple core that someone tossed. She shoved it whole into her mouth and then smiled as if she couldn't believe her incredible fortune. Then there was a man and a woman in fancy clothes. The woman, who wore an elaborate hat, was looking over a table of jewelry and strings of what appeared to be teeth or perhaps small bones. They each had cloth masks over their mouths. As the woman examined a necklace, the man kept looking around as if expecting someone.

Other stalls and shops sold beaten-up appliances, televisions, radios, computers, mobicoms, and other gadgets that Joe had never seen before. There were also displays of organ scaffolds and exoskeletons. Storefronts proclaimed services for gene mapping, modification, and splicing, as well as fresh replacement organs. Stores sold live animal cells and stem cells. Pet shops sold exotic hybrids like flying cats and miniature chimps with human vocal cords, while other places carried drugs for physical and mental enhancement.

To Joe, it was all a blur of bizarre things he barely understood or wanted to understand.

"Stay close to me," Phil said.

It wasn't hard to keep up with him because Phil walked very leisurely. He sidestepped people who suddenly appeared in his way. He said, "Pardon me" as he shuffled around a clot of people who were blocking his path. Joe kept smelling food from restaurants and vendors and wondered why they weren't stopping. They passed close by a cart strung with the dead carcasses of birds, rats, rabbits, and spotted hogs, which apparently Phil didn't see because he didn't stop, so Joe grabbed his sleeve.

"Hey," Joe said. "There's food right here."

"That's no good," Phil said. "I know where you can get food at a good price. It's up ahead."

What Joe saw around the corner didn't make him feel very confident. The street was more like an alley, dark and deserted. Along the center of the cracked and crumbled cobblestones was a stream of slimy water, and along the edges were heaps of moldering garbage against the sides of the black buildings. Near the end of the street, on the right hand side, was a faint halo of ruddy light.

"I don't see anything down there," Joe said.

"See that light? That's it. The best biscuits in the whole city."

"I don't know."

"Come now. Trust me."

That was the problem. The queer feeling from earlier got worse. He knew this was a bad idea. He could hear Frank saying, "If you feel afraid, be afraid." Only he doubted himself. He wasn't sure the queer feeling was fear. Maybe it was just nerves, or maybe it was hunger. After all, if Phil was right, Joe would get the food he needed for Mary and the baby. He was sure he could escape if he had to. Just a little bit further, he thought.

Halfway down the squalid street, Joe saw two pairs of feet wrapped in rags sticking out of a wood crate between mounds of trash. The sight startled him and he slipped on the slick cobblestones and stepped into the slimy stream of water.

"You okay?" Phil asked.

"Somebody's there," Joe said.

"They're dead. Keep going."

"How do you know they're dead?"

"They're dead. They're urchins. Don't waste your time. They might as well be dead. Come on."

Up the dark street, Joe heard voices. Two stumbling figures appeared like shadows against the dim light shining from the street behind them. Water splashed and a tin can clunked on the ground. The two men passed under the glow of the ruddy light in the alley. They wore thick wool caps and frayed jackets with no shirts underneath. Their pants were ripped and tattered at the ends and one man, who appeared drunker than the other, was missing a shoe. He laughed and staggered to his knees. The other man fumbled for him and finally caught hold of his collar and yanked him to his feet.

"They might be faking it," Phil said. "They might want us to think they're drunk, so they can rob us. Slow down. Stay close to me."

Phil grabbed Joe's arm and they practically came to a halt as they waited for the drunken men to pass safely by.

"You can never be too careful," Phil said. But in the next moment, he said, "Did you hear that?"

Joe perked up his ears and tried to listen for any unusual sounds. He didn't hear anything. He looked behind him. The drunken men were out of sight now. He looked at the ruddy light shining ahead where Phil said the biscuits where at. He didn't see anything strange up there either.

"I thought I heard the sound of an Arbyter." Phil looked around. "They might be conducting a sweep. Over here," he said. "There's a place to hide."

Phil latched onto Joe, and before Joe knew what happened or even had a chance to protest, Phil pulled him into a dark entryway. He felt Phil's warm breath next to his ear, and then something wet, like the first raindrops to fall before a storm. Joe went to wipe it away, but his hand brushed against Phil's lips.

Phil breathed heavily. He seized Joe's hand and pressed his lips to Joe's knuckles.

"Stop," Joe said. He tried to rip his hand free. "What are you doing?"

Phil clenched Joe's wrist with one hand while he wedged his forearm against Joe's throat. The back of Joe's head grated on the brick wall behind him. He didn't understand what was happening. Then Phil released his wrist, and Joe tried to shove him away, only Phil slammed into him and jammed his hand down into Joe's pants.

"Stop," Joe tried to shout.

Then Joe swung his foot up in the air as hard as he could and slammed it right between Phil's legs. Phil let go, stumbled backwards, and doubled over. He groaned and gasped for breath. When Joe saw him fall, he didn't waste any time. He whipped around the corner, slipping on the wet stones before he was able to catch his footing again.

He ran several blocks, turning down different dark streets, until he finally slowed to a stop and looked behind him. Phil wasn't there. Joe ducked into a tight crevice between two buildings. He bent over at the waist and braced his hands against his knees. His chest was heaving like something alive was in it. He couldn't catch his breath, and he thought he was going to vomit. Then his stomach convulsed. It felt like it was turning inside out and it was going to punch through his throat and out his mouth. A moment later he retched, but all that came out was stringy liquid. Nothing solid came out because nothing solid was in his stomach.

Chapter 35

He must've taken a wrong turn somewhere because now he was lost. Earlier, he'd found a house where a slender woman lived. She took mercy on him but at a price. She ended up selling Joe two sausages and half a loaf of bread for his ten shekels. That was all the money they had left. He didn't know if it was a good deal or not, but at that point he didn't care. He simply wanted to get some food, any food, and get back to Mary as soon as possible.

After he got the food, he tried to find his way back to the rooming house using back ways to avoid the Fulfillment District. However, the more he tried to navigate the streets, the more disoriented he got, especially when another rolling blackout came and the streetlights went out. In time he reached the river, even though he didn't know how. He climbed up a bank littered with trash and found a bench beside a scraggly tree. Across the river in the slums were flashes of orange light from small campfires. Joe looked over his shoulder, where the city lay in darkness, except for the Green Zone, where the tall buildings still shined with lights. Apparently not everyone lost power in a blackout.

From the corner of his eye, Joe caught a glint of something. Coming up the river was a boat shining a searchlight around in a circle. It sprayed the dark water and the jagged rooftops of the slums. Joe hid behind the tree and watched the boat slowly approach. He made sure to keep out of sight when the searchlight swung past and splashed the ground around him.

As the boat cruised closer, Joe saw the large cannon mounted on the deck and the tall tower with small yellow windows and a thick blade spinning on top. On the side was the ever-present symbol of the Guardian Party. Joe watched as the searchlight swept across the girders of the bridge in the distance. That's what he wanted to see. He knew if he could get to the bridge, he could follow the streets that they had been on the first day and retrace his way to the rooming house, where he knew, by now, Mary must be panicky because he wasn't back yet.

Along the riverbanks, Joe skirted around some piles of debris. He kept to the banks to avoid running into anyone, especially policemen or soldiers in armored Arbyters. But that became too difficult. He kept slipping and falling and stepping in mush and muck. So he decided to abandon the relative safety of the riverbanks. He scrambled down to the dark street, which turned out to be a bad idea.

A white light exploded in front of him. It stung his eyes and made him stagger to his knees as if someone had struck him. He kept his head buried in the crook of his arm to block out the searing light. Then someone yanked him to his feet by his collar and dragged him to the back of an enclosed truck. Black spots kept blooming and spinning in front of his eyes. Only on the periphery could he get any sense of what was happening. He heard the clunk of metal and the sound of a heavy door swinging open. He was lifted in the air by his collar and tossed into a mass of bodies that punched and kicked him until he was crushed against the side of a wall between two big bodies that jammed sharp elbows into his ribs.

The air was stifling hot and smelled of rancid sweat and alcohol. Joe gathered his knees up tight to his chest and clutched them with his arms to make himself as small and hard as possible. No one spoke. The only sounds were belches and farts and coughs. He noticed he was trembling. It was fear, but it was also anger. He was angry with himself for following Phil when his instincts had been telling him all along that it was a bad idea. How stupid could he be? And now look at him. Worst of all, he was angry about how this was going to affect Mary. The longer he was gone, the more afraid she was going to get. He didn't really care what was going to happen to him. All he could think about was getting back to Mary.

After a while the truck moved. Bodies slammed against him. The truck jounced and rocked over the rough road. His tailbone smacked against the hard floor and sent a shivery stab of pain up his spine. He still couldn't see anything. The darkness was too thick. Someone shoved him and dug their hands in his back pockets where the sausages and bread were and then yanked them out.

"Hey," Joe said.

A hand like a vice clamped over his mouth. He couldn't breathe. Finally, the truck stopped again and the hand let go. The doors swung open and a dim light filled the interior enough that Joe saw a mash of people, both men and woman, turning their faces from the light, except for those people who had black hoods over their heads.

Policeman, dressed all in black with shiny gorgets and helmets, jumped into the truck. They began kicking and jabbing people with rifles to move them toward the exit. The bodies seemed to drop out of the back of the truck like bags. Other policemen on the ground shouted instructions and insults. When they reached Joe, he dodged a rifle butt and scurried to the edge of the truck bed where he leapt into a pile of bodies struggling to get to their feet.

Once again, Joe got shoved to the side. He landed on his arm and then rolled away, but as luck would have it he happened to roll under the truck and out of sight. He lay still for a few seconds, surprised at where he found himself. He thought for sure the policemen would soon find him and jab rifles beneath the truck and shout for him to get out. He watched more bodies hit the ground as policemen grabbed them and hauled them to their feet. All the while no one came after him. In the chaos, no one must've seen him go under the truck.

He realized this could be his chance to escape.

Flat on his stomach, he squirmed toward the front of the truck. As he moved beneath the engine, he accidentally struck his head against its hot metal. He winced, rubbed the top of his head, and then continued until he was directly below the bumper. The shadow from the truck darkened the street in front of him, but off to the sides there was light glowing along the walls of the building. They were in a narrow street. Joe inched forward a little more.

Up ahead was the bottom of what looked like an Arbyter. There was enough clearance that he could scamper beneath and then see if it was possible to make a run for it, provided there was nothing on the other side obstructing his way. All he had to do was make it across ten feet of exposed ground without anyone noticing.

Without a second thought, he bolted out from under the truck, staying crouched as he sprinted furiously to the Arbyter and dove underneath. He raked his chest on the rough ground, tearing a button off his shirt, before he came to a halt and shimmied forward so his legs weren't jutting out. He waited again. When nothing happened, he knew he must've made it without being detected. He crawled on his elbows, swishing his hips to propel himself, until he reached the other end of the Arbyter. As far as he could see, there wasn't another vehicle in front of him. The street looked clear ahead, dark but clear. This time he really had to make a run for it.

He flew out into the open, rising up to his full height. His legs were pumping so hard he thought they would come unhinged. He waited for the shouts of policemen and the blast of guns. His insides clenched-up like a knot, while his body felt like it was shaking and trembling. Then he stumbled. He skidded on his knees and his body whipped forward. He would've smacked his face against the ground if he hadn't stuck his elbow out. It cracked against a sharp stone, ramming his shoulder up into his jaw. It felt like his arm had been wrenched loose.

He twirled around and looked behind him. The Arbyter was cloaked in a shadow. His gut unclenched and now it felt like spilled liquid. Behind the Arbyter was the truck, then a splash of light against the walls of the buildings. He'd made it. High in the air, a faint beacon of light swished across the black sky. It must be a searchlight from a boat on the river, which meant the river was in that direction. That's all he needed to know.

He got up again and ran. He rounded the corner and made his way down the street, and after he turned so he was headed in the direction of the river, he finally slowed his pace. His blood felt like it was speeding around inside his body. He cradled his arm and walked a while in the dark until he came to the crumbled remains of a building where it wasn't as dark. Some of the light from the Green Zone had found its way there and settled on the ruins. He stopped to inspect the damage to his arm. It didn't look broken, but there was a gash on his elbow where his shirt was torn. Blood dripped. He tested his shoulder, shrugged it, rotated it, and was satisfied that it was okay. After rummaging in some nearby garbage, he found a soiled rag. He tied it around his bleeding elbow. He didn't know what time it was, but he knew it had to be very late. Then he remembered the food he'd bought and felt his back pockets in the miraculous hope that the sausages and bread where still there. Of course, they weren't.

Later, he found some more garbage in the back of a tavern with darkened windows. He scrounged around in the trashcans and bags until he found some bones with meat still on them. He also found some shriveled up carrots. He bit a hunk off one and chewed. It would do. He stuffed the food scraps in his pockets and continued on.

Chapter 36

Dawn arrived by the time he got to the rooming house. The darkness thinned as the sun burned through the fog that rolled off of Lake Mashenomak. Joe was exhausted. His legs felt as if they were wading through sludge. He was worried sick that something terrible had happened to Mary. He only wanted to find her safe, and then to rest. He wanted to lie on the bed next to her, close his eyes, and sleep for a long, long time.

When he stepped inside their room, he didn't see her anywhere. She wasn't on the bed or sitting in the chair by the window or standing in front of the fuzzy TV screen. He didn't panic, at least not right away, because he noticed the bathroom door was closed. He thought maybe she was soaking in the bathtub, and she hadn't heard him come in. Joe knocked on the door. He said her name. When no answer came, he turned the knob, pushed the door open, and found the bathroom empty.

"Mary!" he shouted. He ran out into the hallway. "Mary!" he shouted again.

Someone yelled back at him to shut up. Then down at the far end of the hallway, Ava appeared in a violet-colored robe. She motioned with her hand for him to come.

"She's okay," Ava said. "She's in here."

Joe ran down the hall, brushed past Ava, and darted into the room. Mary sat huddled in a plush red chair. Her head was lowered so that it looked like there was only a hat sitting atop her shoulders. Her thin arms crisscrossed her protruding belly as if she was holding it in place. There was the sound of soft scratchy music and the scent of tobacco smoke and lavender lingering in the air.

When Mary lifted her head and saw Joe, she leapt out of the chair and ran to him. She threw her arms around his neck, buried her head against his chest, and clung to him. He felt her belly press against him and her slender body trembling in his arms.

"She was scared out of her mind," Ava said. "She was screaming. They were going to throw her out, but I told them I'd keep her quiet in my room until you got back. *If* you got back."

"Of course I was coming back," Joe said. "I wouldn't leave her."

Mary finally let go and stepped back.

"What happened to you?" Ava said to Joe. "You look like a wreck."

The knees in his pants were torn, a button was missing on his grimy shirt, a blood stained rag was tied around his elbow, and his face was smudged with dirt.

"I went out to look for food, but the police picked me up, and somehow I managed to get away."

"Lucky," Ava said.

"I got something to eat, though."

He dug in his pockets and pulled out the half-eaten bones and the limp carrots.

"You can't eat those," Ava said. "They're rotten. I've got food here. You can have some. The girl already had some bread and jam."

"Jam?" Joe said.

"You can have some too. I'll make some for you. Go in the bathroom and get cleaned up. I have some clothes you can wear."

Joe looked at Mary. He still felt warm and good at finding her safe, but now he wondered if her health was better.

"Is she still sick?" he asked Ava.

"That girl is skin and bones. And she could go into labor at any second. It's a wonder she's in as good a shape as she is. I gave her a little medicine to help. Now go clean up."

In the bathroom, Joe was surprised at how friendly—even motherly—Ava was being, especially after how cold and suspicious she'd been toward him before. He was also glad she'd rescued Mary. She didn't have to do that. After all, they meant nothing to her. For all she knew she could be getting into a host of problems by helping them out.

Joe untied the soiled rag around his elbow. When he pulled it away, the dried blood peeled off with the rag. It stung like being cut all over again. Some blood dribbled down his arm. He stripped off his clothes. He saw the scabbed-over scratches on his legs from when they were attacked in the forest. It seemed ages ago when that happened. Once he filled the sink with water, he took a washcloth off a rod and picked up a bar of soap in a dish and washed himself all over. The water in the basin turned blackish-gray with dirt. He ran the soap over the cut on his elbow.

Then the door opened and Joe grabbed a towel to cover himself.

"Here's the clothes," Ava said. She must've caught his startled look because she added, "You don't have anything I haven't seen before." But she didn't leave after that. "Let me take care of that cut," she said.

"That's okay," Joe said. He tied the towel around his waist.

"No, it's not okay. It'll get infected if not done right."

There wasn't much Joe could say. She seemed dead-set on helping him. After she opened a cabinet, she pulled out a small bottle and unscrewed the cap. She wrapped her fingers around his skinny forearm and turned it to see his elbow. He must've flinched a little because Ava said, "Hold still. I'm not going to hurt you."

She poured a few drops from the bottle onto his cut, which burned and made him suck his teeth before the burn went away. Then Ava dabbed it with a cloth. Joe watched her attentively. He noticed the faint lines fanning out from the corners of her eyes and the little creases like water ripples at the sides of her mouth. She looked older now that he saw her up close. He smelled the cigarette smoke on her breath, peppery and sweet at the same time, and he smelled the lavender coming from her hair.

"Why are you being so nice to us?"

"A person needs a reason to be nice?"

"No, I was just wondering because of the way you acted before."

"That's just a front I put on to protect myself."

"So you're not really like that?"

"Cynical, you mean?"

He didn't know if that's what he meant or not. He didn't know what "cynical" was.

"I've always been a bit leery," she continued. "It's my personality. I'm sure they weren't expecting that little glitch when they designed me. I'm not artificial or synthetic or anything like that." She paused for a second. "Do you have any idea what I'm talking about? Do you know what a GeM is?"

Joe remembered Frank talking about people in the Green Zone who were "enhanced" and called themselves "transhuman." Frank didn't really understand it all. It was just stuff he heard about but never really witnessed. Joe didn't know if that was what Ava was referring to or not. He didn't want to appear dumb if he was wrong, so he didn't say anything.

"Let me put it this way," she said. "I was created in a laboratory. Genetically modified, altered, mixed, whatever you want to call it. They used specific genes, so I'd be a certain way. It's basically crossbreeding, the same thing you do with plants and animals but at a more sophisticated level. Anyway, my real name isn't Ava. It's GeM X7-391."

Joe was curious now. "But you're still human, right?"

She laughed. "Yes, I'm still human. Which is part of the problem. That's why they fast-tracked the creation of Amalgams that are more programmable. Part computer, part human."

"But they look human?"

"You wouldn't know the difference."

"So what were you made for?"

"To serve top officials in government and industry, in particular the head of the Ministry of Peace and Security."

Joe remembered that title. "Is he the same man I saw on TV?"

"That's him. Scaring everybody with the terrorist bogeyman."

"What happened?"

"I didn't like him. I couldn't stand him really, and one day I said screw it. I refused to service him. So I was expelled. I was renamed, retagged, and dumped in the Fulfillment District with a suitcase and a hundred shekels. Luckily, part of my training included dance. And I'm good at it. That's how I get by these days."

Ava finished cleaning the cut and grabbed a piece of gauze out of the cabinet. She pressed it on his elbow and tied a string around it to secure it.

"That's better," she said.

When she looked at Joe, he realized she'd caught him staring at her. He looked away, but not before he saw her grin. It wasn't a full grin, though, or even particularly genuine; it seemed half-hearted at best.

After Ava left the bathroom, he put on the white pullover shirt she'd given him. It didn't have any buttons down the front. And then he slipped on the brown pants. The clothes were baggy, but they were better than his raggedy old ones. He felt sort of funny not wearing a green button-up shirt like he always wore. He grabbed his pocketknife, the empty coin purse, and the three bullets out of his old clothes and stuffed them in the pockets of his new pants.

When he came out of the bathroom, he looked at Mary. As usual, she had her head down and he really couldn't see her.

Joe spread his arms out and said to her, "What do you think?" Mary didn't answer. "You are going to spoil me with all your compliments."

Ava held a tray with slices of brown bread and a glass jar of red jam. She set the tray on a table in the corner where there were two chairs. Joe sat down across from Ava as she spread some jam on a piece of bread.

Now that Joe felt more at ease, he realized that Ava's room had electricity, and the scratchy music was coming from a big radio standing in the corner.

"There's a blackout," Joe said. "How're you getting power?"

"I have a battery for emergencies," she said. "It cost me a hell of a lot, too."

When she handed the slice of bread to him, she caught him staring again. One side of her mouth curled up into what he thought was going to be a smile, but it turned out to be only a half-smile, or perhaps it was another half-hearted attempt at a smile or not a smile at all. Maybe it was just another sign of her doubt that anything was truly what it appeared to be.

"You hungry?" she said.

"Starving," Joe said.

He took a big bite and never tasted anything so good. The bread was firm and the jam sweet. It tickled his tongue.

"You like it?" she asked.

"It's delicious."

"Raspberry."

Ava glanced at Mary, who was sitting in the plush chair again.

"She doesn't talk," Ava said.

"She does once she gets to know you. But even then she doesn't say a lot."

"What did you say her name was? Mary?"

"That's what I call her. I tried to get her name but she wouldn't tell me, so I had to give her one." Joe took another bite of bread and jam. "I don't know what her real name is."

"You don't know her real name, but she's having your baby?"

Joe realized how that sounded, especially in light of the story he'd told Ava when they first met. He chewed and swallowed.

"She's an orphan. She never had a name."

"Are you two married?"

"Of course."

"No rings?"

"I don't have money for something like that."

He hoped his answers satisfied her, but when she looked at him, one eye narrowed while the other eye widened, as if she were peering through a keyhole to see if someone was really on the other side.

"You should take her to a hospital," Ava said.

"I will, when she's ready."

"I think she's ready now. Isn't that why you came here?"

"Yes."

"Just take her, then. Take her to the public ward."

"Is she okay?"

"She could go any day. Take her. There's no point in waiting."

"I will," Joe said.

"I don't believe you," Ava said. "What are you hiding?"

"Nothing," Joe said.

"Don't give me that. You can't lie well, so don't even try."

"I'm not."

"You're not? Then why are you staying at a place that's not even close to the hospital? And why are you out driving in that piece of crap wagon all day and gone all night? That looks like somebody who's not telling the truth, and who's up to no good."

"I'm not up to anything."

"Who sent you?"

"Sent me?"

"I'm not buying your dirt-eater act one bit. Who are you working for? Is this a set-up?"

"No. It's nothing like that."

"I hope you're right."

"I am right," Joe said. "I thought you were going to be nice to us."

"Being nice is a luxury."

"Do we really look like trouble to you?"

"The devil always looks innocent. That's why he's the devil."

"I think we need to go now," Joe said.

Joe took three big bites and then crammed the rest of the bread and jam in his mouth so his cheeks bulged.

"I'm only looking out for my interests," she said.

Joe's mouth was too full to say anything. He got up to grab Mary, but Ava caught his arm.

"Hold on," she said. "I didn't mean to upset you. I don't know if you're up to anything or not. It's just in my nature to see the dark side in everything."

He swallowed the hunk of food in his mouth. "We should still go," he said. "It's been a long night."

The look in Ava's eyes made Joe think she might be sincere, which surprised him. Ava let him loose and he went to Mary and leaned over her. He grasped her thin hand and helped her to her feet. When he turned around, he half expected Ava to say they didn't have to leave, especially after what she just said. He might've reconsidered leaving, but in the end she didn't say anything. In fact, she didn't even look at them.

On their way out, Joe said, "Thanks for helping us."

He meant it too.

Chapter 37

Back in their room, Joe tried the light switch but there was still no power. He forgot it was morning outside and all he needed to do was open the curtains. Instead, he found the candles in the cabinet and lit them with a box of matches from the drawer. He didn't realize his mistake until after he stuffed the matches in his pocket and turned around. Mary had pulled open the curtains and now stood facing the bright sunlit window. For a moment a blur of yellow light outlined her body. After she moved away, Joe saw dark spots floating in front of his eyes.

He didn't know what to think about what just happened with Ava. Should he be nervous about her sudden suspicions or not? He tried to brush it off. He told himself that she'd fallen from her formerly high position and had no power to harm them now. Or did she? Maybe she still had connections. Maybe she was engaged in something illegal herself, and that's why she got so suspicious.

"We have to go and find Templeton right now," he said to Mary, "and sell the diesel so we can get out of here."

He paused. Mary sat in the chair by the window. Her knees were apart to accommodate her belly and her hands were sunk in her dress between her little stick legs. She looked so vulnerable, so delicate. Even though he knew she was stronger than she looked, there was still a part of her that was a frightened girl inside. He realized he needed to calm down. More than likely he was overreacting and making Mary worry for no reason.

"Maybe we should rest before we go," he said.

He smelled lavender again and he figured the scent must've followed them from Ava's room. But when he stepped closer to Mary, he realized the smell was coming from her.

"Did she give you perfume?"

Mary nodded. She held out her wrists for him to sniff. He bent over, lowered his nose to her skin, and breathed in a heady bloom of lavender.

"That's nice," he said.

"She let me put some jewelry on, too."

"I bet you felt rich then."

"No. I didn't want it on."

"It was a rough night, for both of us," he said. "I'm sorry I scared you. I didn't mean for all this stuff to happen. I'm glad I'm back, and you're safe, and we're together again. The rest we'll just have to deal with."

When Mary didn't say anything, he thought maybe she was upset with him.

"You're not mad, are you?" he asked.

"No," she said. "I'm glad you're okay."

"That's good." He remembered what Ava said about Mary being ready to go any day. "How is the baby?" he asked. "Do you need to go to the hospital?"

"Everything is fine," she said.

"You sure? You're not just saying that? You'd tell me if something was wrong?"

"Yes."

He finally sat down on the edge of the bed facing Mary in the chair. He stared at her, at her frail little body carrying that big stomach that held another frail life inside it. At that moment, he wondered if the baby would be a boy or a girl. He wondered what its name would be. What would Mary name her baby? Would she name it after him if it was a boy? Would she name it Joe? Or maybe she would name it after the father?

"Have you picked any names for the baby?"

"You name him."

"Him? You think it's a boy?"

"It feels like a boy."

"How do you know?"

"I just do."

"But he's yours. You should name him, not me."

"I want you to name him."

"What about the father's name?"

She didn't respond right away, and Joe realized that he hadn't asked an innocent question.

"You don't have to answer that, if you don't want to," Joe said.

She raised her head a bit as if she was going to say something. Joe waited for her to speak, but it was hard to keep quiet. He wanted to prompt her.

"The father is my father," she finally said.

Joe didn't understand. He thought she meant the father was the father, which didn't make any sense because it was redundant. Obviously the father was the father.

"I don't know what you mean? The father is my…"

Then he got it. When he heard the exact words coming out of his mouth, he recognized the one word that made all the difference. Immediately, his mind seemed to seize-up. He couldn't think.

"You don't like me anymore?" she said.

"What?"

He still couldn't think. He had a hard time getting his head around it. *The father is her father.*

"You don't like me," she repeated.

"No," Joe said. "Don't say that. Of course I still like you. Nothing's changed. That doesn't matter."

"It doesn't?"

"No."

Joe didn't know if it mattered or not. All he knew was that he cared about Mary. He already figured the baby was a product of something bad. He just didn't expect it to be what she told him.

"Of course it doesn't matter," he continued. "Is that what you were afraid of? Don't worry. I mean it. Nothing will come between us."

"Nothing?"

"Nothing," he repeated. "Remember, everything is washed away. The past is cleansed. You're pure, white as sheep's wool. Remember?"

Then she did something wonderful. She lifted the brim of her hat to look directly into Joe's eyes. The bright morning light flowed over her face. Her eyes seemed to gleam like crystals shining in the sun.

"You are mine," she said.

"Yes, I'm yours," he said.

His reassurance helped her open up. She finally told him where she had come from. Her family had lived much farther south in a small community on the edge of the swamplands. A disease had killed their animals and then began to appear among the people. Her father became increasingly desperate and filled with rage until he went mad. He killed her mother and then killed himself. Mary left the community with a small group that went looking for a better life up north. But the group split into two when some people wanted to go to the city, and others like Mary wanted to find another community who would accept them. They didn't make it far before they were attacked. Only Mary and an old man named Lucius survived. They continued on until they came to the tiny rundown village of Gunther near Joe's family's farm. They stopped at the one room Temple of Virid, where Lucius said that he couldn't take care of the girl and her baby too. That's all he said and left her there. Mom agreed to take her in before she even discussed it with Dad, but Dad wouldn't have denied her anyway. Frank didn't like it. Joe wasn't so happy either. But all that had changed. Everything was different now.

Chapter 38

In the afternoon, they went out to find the fat man, Templeton. This time Joe parked the wagon down the street next to a warehouse and waited for the motorized security cart to go by before he drove the wagon around the side of the steel mill and stopped again beside the back door where they had been yesterday.

"Okay," Joe said. "Remember what we talked about. What do you do if anybody comes?"

"Drive the wagon away and go to where we stopped to look at the lake."

"Right. And then I will meet you there, okay? I won't be long. In a short time, we'll be going home."

He grabbed Mary's hand and squeezed it before he got out and she slid over to where the reins hung slack.

Inside the steel mill, amid the roaring noise and the boiling furnaces, Joe had no problem spotting the fat man. He stood near the second furnace, his thumbs stuck in the sides of his black bib overalls. His fat belly hung down over his waist like an appendage. He watched the greasy grimy men swivel an iron funnel around to pour molten liquid into the casting molds spread out on the floor.

"Hello!" Joe shouted over the noise.

The fat man pivoted slowly. His giant belly slid around, pushing Joe back, making him stumble until he was several feet away from where he started. The fat man stared down at Joe like he was a speck on the ground. His dark eyes flickered with reflected orange light. Tears pooled in his lower lids as if at any second they might spill. It looked as if he was on the verge of weeping, but he didn't. He chomped on a black cigar stub.

"We don't take day labor," he said.

"Templeton?" Joe said.

"Who wants to know?"

"You know Frank?"

"Frank who?"

"Frank from the plains."

The fat man stared, saliva building on his oily lips. Then he smiled.

"The dirt-eater! How could I forget? I yanked him away from that slag wagon, but not before he lost a few fingers."

He clapped Joe on the back and Joe caught a whiff of what smelled like charred toast. It was hard to believe this giant glob of a man was the hero who saved Frank.

"Are you a relative?"

"His brother."

"His brother? Did he send you here instead of coming himself? What a coward."

"My brother is not a coward," Joe said.

"I stand corrected. It's easy to be brave from a distance."

Joe wasn't sure what he meant by that.

"Frank said you would know what to do."

"About what?"

Joe was afraid to say the word. "Some special fuel," he said.

"Special?"

Templeton winked at him in an exaggerated way before he narrowed his eyes. The fiery light reflecting in them dimmed. His eyes turned to what looked like slivers of rubber shaved from a black tire. The tears hanging on his lower eyelids bulged but still didn't spill.

"Alright, little man. Show me what you got."

When they went outside and Templeton saw Mary in the cab, his eyes lit up and he chewed his cigar stub faster, which made his lips even oilier.

"She's a tiny one," he said. "Fresh from the country and pregnant to boot." This seemed to excite him even more. He rubbed his hands and his big belly quivered.

"Allow me, my dear," he said.

He wrapped his thick paws around Mary and lifted her out of the cab. Joe didn't like how Templeton was acting toward her. After he set her on the ground beside the wagon, he withdrew his fat paws from around her body, but not before trailing a dirty claw up her skinny legs and beneath her dress. Mary pushed her dress down against his finger and Templeton laughed.

"Keep your hands off her," Joe said.

"No offense. Don't want me handling the merchandise, huh?"

"She's not the merchandise," he said indignantly. Why did everyone keep thinking that? Instead of getting angry, though, he managed to stay focused. "I got it hidden in the cab."

Joe stepped inside and yanked up the floorboards. He untied the bundle, peeled back the layers of crusty deerskins, and unscrewed the cap on the plastic container of diesel.

"Nice disguise," Templeton said.

It was the first time Joe had seen the diesel since he and Frank poured it into the container back home. A fluttery feeling of excitement came over him when he realized this was the moment for which he and Mary had traveled all these miles for. It was finally here. He was about to fulfill his mission of selling the diesel, exactly what he'd envisioned back home when they first discovered it. The smell of the released fumes spread against his face and made the inside of his nose feel burned.

Templeton grunted as he bent over his huge gut and squeezed his shoulders into the cab. He lowered his head and sniffed.

"Grade A stuff," he said. He stared at Joe. "I won't ask you where you got this."

Joe looked away.

"The SRF hit a refinery the other week, or at least that's what officials are saying, and fuel is in even shorter supply than usual. This will bring a big price."

Joe got out of the cab and stood beside the wagon next to Mary. Templeton's shadow covered them. He eyed Mary again.

"I'm going to make you a generous offer, since you're the dirt-eater brother of one-fingered Frank." He laughed. "Ten thousand shekels," he said, "and the girl."

"What?"

"The girl included."

"Included? No."

"She's seriously not for sale?" Templeton sounded surprised.

"Of course not."

"Not even for an hour?"

Joe looked at Mary. Her head drooped forward in her big floppy hat. She held her fingers laced beneath her distended belly like she was holding a heavy sack. She toed the cinders with her torn-up shoes. He couldn't imagine ever being without her. In fact, he was now furious that Templeton would still think she was part of the bargain. The whole idea disgusted him.

Joe looked back at Templeton. "Not on your life, you ninny shit."

Templeton's eyes narrowed. Joe steeled himself for some kind of assault. The tears hanging in Templeton's eyes seemed about to fall, but yet again they didn't. He spit his cigar at Joe. The slimy stub smacked him in the face and then plopped on the ground. Joe figured that wasn't the end of it. He positioned his foot in preparation to kick Templeton in the crotch like he did to Phil. But that's not what happened. Instead, Templeton eased back on his heels and smiled in a sly way. He leered at Mary. Then he pulled a long cigar from his overalls and shoved it between his oily lips.

"You drive a hard bargain. I can see you are a man of resolve. So I'm willing to offer you five thousand flat."

He rolled the cigar in his mouth. The cigar tip slid around in his lips until it was coated with saliva and turned black. He seemed to think he had made a deal too impossible to resist. And he was right. It was far less than the original offer, but what choice did Joe have now? His brother Frank said to take whatever he gives you. "I don't care how much it is," he'd said. "Even if it's not a lot, or not what we hoped for, take it anyway. Got that?

Just take it and go. Don't mess around." Before Joe could agree to the terms, he heard the buzz of the motorized cart. It was rolling toward them, its red light swiveling on top.

"Damn it," Templeton muttered, and bit down on the cigar.

Joe looked at the exposed container of diesel. The last thing he wanted was to be caught with illegal fuel. He quickly grabbed the floorboards and smacked them down into place. He wondered if he should get in the wagon and start moving. They could always come back again. Now that he'd made contact with Templeton, he'd certainly not want the deal to die. So Joe grabbed Mary by the hand and pulled her toward the cab.

"Hold on," Templeton said. "Don't go anywhere."

The cart came to a stop and the same man from yesterday stepped out. He hitched up his pants, straightened his shirt, and walked forward.

"Ah, Sal," Templeton said. "Good to see you. Protecting us from thieves and saboteurs as always."

"Cut the crap," Sal said. "What's going on?"

"Suspicion always haunts the guilty mind," Templeton said.

"Cut the crap, I said. What's going on?"

"Meet my new friends."

"I met them yesterday."

"I see," Templeton said.

"Anything I should know about?" Sal said. He stared at Templeton as if he expected something.

"Of course, of course."

Templeton dug in his pocket and pulled out a wad of bills.

"You could be a little more subtle," Sal said.

"No need to be ashamed. Business is business."

"Yeah, business that could get me killed." He tipped his head toward the sky. "Eyes in the sky," he said. "Eyes in the sky."

Joe glanced up to see what Sal was talking about, but Joe didn't notice anything until he saw a black globe atop the far corner of the steel mill. He remembered seeing other black globes throughout the city, and he wondered if that's what Sal meant by "eyes in the sky."

Sal looked around a moment before he settled his gaze on Joe. The way Sal stared at him made Joe feel like he was being searched like a criminal.

"You didn't see a thing, right?" Sal said to Joe. "Right?" he repeated. The tone of his voice made it clear there was only one correct answer.

"Right," Joe said.

"Leave it in the usual place," Sal said to Templeton.

After that, Sal turned around, walked to the cart, and got in.

As Sal drove away, Templeton muttered, "Asshole," while he waved his hand. He looked at Joe again. "Now where were we?"

"You were about to give me five thousand."

"Not so fast there. I just had to give up some money to keep this deal alive." He stopped and scratched his chin. "Let's see, how about we meet at the Weimar Club at ten. We'll have a few drinks, watch a show, and do some business."

After Templeton gave Joe the directions, he offered to help Mary back into the cab, but she quickly turned on him before he put a hand on her and stepped into the cab herself.

Templeton laughed. "She's got spunk. I like that. Makes it more fun. Bring her along."

Joe wanted to rip Templeton's repulsive face off.

"She's not coming."

"You could make oodles of money off her, but it's your choice. You kids take care for now."

Templeton winked and then turned and went back in the steel mill. As much as Joe disliked him, there wasn't much he could do about it. He had to play along in order to get the money. That was one of the unsavory parts of life. Sometimes you had to give in to things you hated to, things that made you feel bad about yourself, things that made you feel weak, all in order to simply get something you needed.

After Joe got back in the cab, he turned to Mary and said, "We'll have to wait a little longer. We'll still leave tonight, though. I promise. Before we go, I'll get you that dress. Maybe I'll get some peaches or apples, if we can find them."

He heard the whirling whoosh-whoosh-whoosh of a helicraft overhead. Mary stuck her hands inside the brim of her hat to cover her ears. Joe watched the sleek black body of the helicraft pass into view. On its smooth belly between the pivoting rotor-thrusters was the red symbol of the Guardian. The helicraft hovered for moment, swayed to the right, and then flew away in the distance along with the noise.

As they drove away, his thoughts drifted toward home. He thought of how much he missed it and of how much he wanted to get back. He thought about their hardscrabble farm near the river, where the sky was clear and the land hushed and the air dusty but sweet. He didn't care that they barely survived by scraping what they could from the hard dry earth, and he didn't care that dust storms swept over them, killing off their livestock and burying their crops while they hid in the cellar for the black dusters to pass. It didn't matter now.

That was his home. That was their home. That was Mary and the baby's home. With that money, as long as it lasted, he and Frank could go on buying expeditions every year and get all the family needed to survive.

He looked at Mary. He imagined her sitting on the back deck that he was going to build for her when they got back home. He could see it all clearly. He would step out of the barn, after milking the dairy cow they bought with the money, and see her sitting on the deck, rocking the baby in a chair. He would see the endless blue sky behind her and the sun shining on her like an angel. It was a perfect vision, and he couldn't wait to experience it for real.

He planned to do a lot of things now; a lot of building and repairs that his parents never bothered with because secretly they thought it was useless. Although they never said that, their actions and demeanor made it obvious that they had given up hope. But imagine their reaction after he and Mary returned after being gone so long. Just imagine it. They'd be so happy to see them alive that they'd forget about how he and Mary had snuck away in the dark of night. His parents would forget all about the weeks and weeks of worry and fear that their youngest boy and adopted girl were lost and never coming back. Imagine the welcome. Imagine their surprise when he showed them all the money, the money that would bring hope back into their lives. And imagine the pride in Frank's eyes.

Chapter 39

That night, before he went to meet Templeton at the Weimar Club, Mary tugged on his arm. She asked if she could come with him, but it was too dangerous this time. He knew she didn't want to be left alone, especially after the other night. He also knew she was afraid he wouldn't come back again, so he told her that it wouldn't take long. It was a simple transaction. She would hardly know he was gone. He told her to think about the money and how that meant they could all be together for a very long time. When that didn't satisfy her completely, he continued. He told her that at the first sign of trouble he would leave, and that he wouldn't risk anything if it meant they wouldn't be together. That seemed to work.

He left the horses and wagon in the stable because he was too afraid of leaving them somewhere unattended in the Fulfillment District. His plan was to bring Templeton back to the stable and give him the diesel there. Even though he was sure Templeton wouldn't like that, Joe didn't really care. He dreaded seeing him again, but it was a necessary evil. Five thousand shekels was nothing to sneeze at. It wasn't a huge fortune, not like the initial ten thousand, but if they were smart, it could last a good long time.

When he finally stepped inside the Weimar Club, his attention was immediately drawn to the stage. A small band of strings and brass played raucously as naked women painted in assorted colors cavorted around another woman who was unpainted. That woman was writhing around and spreading her hands all over herself. Joe knew he shouldn't stare, but it was all he could seem to do. The rest of the big room was filled with tables of people drinking, smoking, and shouting. The air was clouded with white smoke. On a balcony were more women—strumpets, no doubt—with open tops and loose hair. They stood in front of doors where disheveled men stumbled in and out.

Templeton wasn't hard to spot. He sat in the corner, like a giant rubbish pile, puffing on a cigar and clutching a stein of beer. Next to him were two strumpets with their blouses open and halfway off their shoulders.

When Templeton spotted Joe, he shouted, "Dirt-eater!"

Joe weaved through the mess of people until he was in front of Templeton's table. His eyes were still filled with those tears that never fell. His white shirt was stained black with drool. The strumpets leaned against his massive body like they were leaning against a tower of rotting mattresses. They looked at Joe with glassy eyes and dull smiles. Their cheeks were rouged with pink circles and their eyelids coated in blue shadow. One of them had a gap in her front teeth.

"Wasn't sure you would show," Templeton said. "How do you like my accessories?"

He enveloped each woman in his heavy arms and shook them so their breasts bounced. Templeton laughed. Joe looked away and sat on a wood chair across the table.

"What about the deal?" Joe said.

"Deal? What deal?" he laughed. "We'll talk business later. Now it's time for fun. Where is that girl of yours? Don't tell me you didn't bring her?"

"I don't want any fun. I just want to go. What do we need to do?"

"Slow down! You need to learn how to relax. Pleasure is peace, my friend."

"I don't care. I want what's mine."

"Nothing's yours until I say it's yours. You get it when I'm good and ready. What else are you going to do? Who else are you going to go to?"

"I can find someone else."

"Really? Where? How?"

"I don't know. I'll figure it out."

"One false move and you're dead. Matter of fact, I could alert the authorities about you right now. There are more desperate losers out there besides you. It's what keeps me in the money. Go ahead, walk away, if you got all the answers, if you're such a big man, go ahead. Go. I dare you."

Joe stared at Templeton. His watery eyes were full of smug glee, which only made Joe angrier and want to prove the fat beast wrong. He wanted to spit in his eyes and walk away.

"Awfully quiet," Templeton said. "You don't have any other choice. So don't do something stupid."

Joe slumped in his chair and accepted that he would have to put up with whatever Templeton wanted. He remembered the teachings of the Prophet Roy, who said, "The humble spirit grows strong" and "Only the meek find rest" and "Walk the earth as if you are air." They were words he often found himself rebelling against, but now they provided the fortitude he needed to deal with Templeton.

"Ah, she's here!" Templeton called out. "The loveliest dancer of them all."

Joe turned to see who he was talking about. To his shock, he saw Ava sauntering toward their table. She wore a pale blue robe that billowed around her legs. Her hair was swept to one side and fell across her breast. He realized that she must've been one of the dancers on stage, but he never noticed her up there. He couldn't picture which one she had been. Then it dawned on him. She was the one in the middle, the one that the painted girls were dancing around.

She appeared to be as shocked to see Joe as he was to see her. When their eyes met, she hesitated a moment as a flash of recognition ran across her face. But after that she acted very cool. She pulled the chair out beside Joe and nodded her head at him as if meeting him for the first time. She sat down. Joe shifted uncomfortably.

"Let me introduce you to my new colleague," Templeton said, gesturing toward Joe.

Ava didn't turn to him to shake his hand or acknowledge the introduction. He interpreted her indifference as hostility, especially after what happened in her room. What he wondered was how she knew Templeton. Or more to the point, *why* she knew him? To Joe, Templeton was disgusting and lecherous, so why would anyone want to willingly be associated with him?

Joe watched Ava take a silver case out of the side pocket in her robe, set it on the table, and flip it open to reveal a neat row of white cigarettes. She slipped one out, closed the case, tapped the end on the top of the case and slid the cigarette between her lips. Templeton suddenly lurched forward, rocking the table with the roll of his flesh as he struck a match. The end of the match disappeared in his fat fingers as he extended the tiny flame to ignite Ava's cigarette. When he sat back with another lurch, the table rocked again.

"You were marvelous as always," Templeton declared. "Come, sit by me."

He callously pushed away the two half-dressed strumpets to clear a space for him to lavish attention on Ava. As the other woman stumbled away, Ava blew out some smoke, picked her case up off the table, and got to her feet.

"I only have a few minutes," she said, "before I have to get ready for the next show."

"Of course, of course," Templeton said.

Ava shuffled around the table and eased into the chair next to Templeton. He looked as if he wanted to engulf her. His wet, slippery lips trembled.

"You know the deal," she said.

"Yes, of course."

He plunged his hand into his hip pocket, dug around, and pulled out some bills that he set on the table in front of Ava. Joe had never seen paper shekels before. They only came in fifties and hundreds. There appeared to be several bills there, but he didn't get a chance to see how much before Ava stashed them in her robe. Templeton then leaned toward her. His eyes fluttered, his nostrils flared as he breathed her in. He let out a purring sound that bubbled at his wet lips. The sight made Joe cringe, but Ava didn't seem to be bothered at all. It didn't look like the first time this had happened, especially when Templeton slithered his arm around her shoulders. He curled his hand like a fat claw across the top of her breast and caressed the bottom of her chin with a thick stumpy finger. Once again Ava took it all in stride.

"Why won't you be mine?" he said.

"I did that once. And look what it got me."

Templeton chuckled.

"I could set you up far away from here," he said.

"And be a prisoner? I already did that too."

"I'm not going to be in this game much longer. I've got enough to get free now."

"And give up your pleasures and power? You couldn't leave if you wanted to."

"I can do whatever I want."

"Only because they look the other way and get a cut. Don't fool yourself. They won't want to lose their piggy bank or want their piggy bank to squeal."

"You shouldn't talk to me like that."

"You shouldn't talk like an idiot."

"Who's going to touch me? I'm invincible." He threw out his arms and puffed out his chest to show his invincibility before hunching over Ava again. "Like you said, they don't want to lose their piggy bank."

"Unless they find another one and you become disposable."

He paused a moment, as if mulling over what she said, before saying, "What do you know?"

"Nothing. It's hypothetical. All I'm saying is you aren't exactly discreet."

"You do know something."

"Only what I see."

"Don't tease me. Tell me what you know."

"I think I've made my point." She nodded at Joe without looking at him. "You think he's deaf and can't hear what we're talking about?"

As she was saying that, Joe felt something nudge his foot and then tap his toes. He stared at Ava, but she didn't make any sign that it was her, although it had to be her. He wasn't sure what she meant by it. Maybe it was just to acknowledge him, or maybe it was to warn him.

"Him? A dirt-eater?" Templeton chortled. "Don't make me laugh."

"That's exactly what I mean." Ava said. "Don't get comfortable. You have rivals who want to clear the way."

"Clear the way?"

"You know what I mean."

"No one has the balls to take me out."

"Have you forgotten about Red?"

"Red is a punk."

"He might be a punk, but he's smart enough to see a chance."

"Stop messing with me. You trying to make me paranoid?"

"I'm trying to save your ass."

"By making me jumpy?"

"By making you see that conditions have changed."

"So you are trying to warn me."

"Take it any way you want. I have to go soon."

"You can't just leave me hanging like this."

Ava didn't say anything. She sucked in deeply on her cigarette and blew the smoke out slowly. The white tip was smudged with lipstick. Finally, she looked at Joe, but only briefly. He could see in her eyes that she was even more suspicious of him than before.

Chapter 40

Ava put her cigarette case in her robe and was about to leave when two men in black hoods darted out of the crowd. They swooped in with long knifes that glinted beneath the lights. At first, Joe didn't fully comprehend what was happening. Only after they grabbed the heads of Ava and Templeton and yanked them back did Joe understand. By that time, however, it was too late. The sharp blades sliced deep into both of their necks. The blood squirted. It shot out like water from a punctured hose.

The blood hit Joe and he toppled over backwards in his chair. On the floor, he wiped his blood-spattered face with his sleeve, and even though he should've stayed down, he scrambled to his feet again. His left eye was cloudy and burned from the blood that got in it, but he could still see well enough to know that several more men in black hoods had descended from out of nowhere. They stabbed Templeton's fat body like a flock of ravens pecking and tearing at a bloated animal. Ava was nowhere in sight. She must've crashed to the floor below the tabletop, which was now a wet puddle of spilled beer and dark blood.

The massacre was seemingly over as violently as it began. The hooded men dashed away into the screaming mob of people gathered around the bloody scene. For a few seconds nothing happened. Then the crowd fell on the murdered bodies like vultures.

Joe went into a full-on alarm. He ducked under the table as it rocked and swayed from the rush of people swarming around. They grabbed and tore at Ava and Templeton's clothes and bodies. They were taking anything they could get. Money was ripped from hand to hand until it was shreds. A siren went off, loud and shrieking. Ava's robe was torn loose, her bare skin scratched and clawed. The table tipped over and feet trampled on Joe. He got tangled for a moment in the thicket of legs before he slid into a tight gap between two people and pushed himself to his feet. He fought his way through the crowd until he reached the door and squeezed outside.

He shimmied along the face of the building to a narrow alley, no bigger than a hallway, and stopped. He saw the flashing red lights of two trucks, and then two Arbyters with their mounted cannons swiveling over the mob.

"Disperse! Disperse!" a loudspeaker proclaimed, followed by a popping sound.

The air filled with bursts of yellow and white smoke. Joe didn't know what it was. The crowd turned frantic as they scattered. Several people, stumbling and coughing, pushed past Joe and knocked him against the wall in the alley. He smelled an acrid odor, and when he breathed, his lungs seized. He thought it must be some kind of poison, so he ran down the alley with the other fleeing people. The wretched smoke continued to follow him. His eyes watered. But he happened to spot a small opening in the brick foundation of the building opposite the Weimar Club. It was either a knocked-out window or knocked-out bricks. Either way, Joe thought he could hide there until everything calmed down.

He dove on the ground and wedged his shoulders between the bricks and squirmed into a dark crawl space. He felt around for something to block the opening and keep the smoke from seeping in. He found something that crinkled when he touched it. It was an old sheet of plastic. He plastered it against the opening and waited.

After he coughed a few more times, his lungs started to clear. Even though he felt safer now, his nerves were still raw. He was still rattled from the savage attack on Templeton and Ava, especially the way Ava's white throat split open and the way her blood gushed out. He thought he heard her gasp softly before the knife cut in and slashed her neck. He remembered her throwing her arms in the air and the V of her robe peeling open to expose the hollow of her neck.

While he lay in the dark crawl space, he wondered what was going to happen now. He didn't know how much more of this he could take until it didn't seem worth it. His only contact to sell the diesel was dead. Then he heard the rapid tat-tat-tat of rifle fire. He flinched and let go of the plastic. The bitter smoke rolled in before he could get the plastic over the opening again. It stung his eyes and throttled his lungs. He gasped for air a few times. The thought flashed through his mind that he could be suffocating, but a moment later his lungs began to inflate again. He coughed and hacked. His eyes watered, so he kept them closed.

Once again, he wondered what he was going to do. If he still wanted to get money for the diesel, he'd have to find another buyer. He was back to square one—worse than square one because he had no idea who to go to next. What about Templeton's rival, Red? It seemed like the only option Joe had left. He had to find Red. But where and how, especially with only one day remaining on their tags?

As bad as that was he had more pressing issues at hand, like who sent the killers and how was Ava involved? Did the killers know who Joe was now? Were they coming after him next? Worse yet, was Mary in danger? Was someone on their way to Mary and Joe's room right then? The only important thing now was to make sure Mary was safe. They had to get out of sight and leave the rooming house. The rest he'd have to sort out later.

Joe tore the plastic away from the opening. He crawled out into the alley and stood up. A whiff of the foul smoke still lingered in the air.

He only made it to the end of the alley before two men grabbed him. They wore long dark coats and fedoras with thin red bands on them. One of them snatched Joe's wrist and scanned it. His face was narrow in the eyes and broader around his jaws. He must've been fond of candy because his breath smelled like peppermint.

"It's him," he said. "It's the dirt-eater."

The other man pulled something out of his pocket. He shoved it in Joe's hand. It was a piece of paper.

"We know you have the diesel," he said. He stared straight into Joe's eyes. "Follow these directions and all will be forgiven."

They let go of him and then walked away as if nothing had happened. Joe slumped against the wall. He looked at the paper in his hand and unfolded it.

It read, "Take the diesel to the old church on Ludwig and 10th. Bring the girl."

Chapter 41

That evening, Joe and Mary set out to find the church. They went through parts of the city where decaying buildings lay and people milled about as if they didn't notice a thing. Joe couldn't stop fidgeting. It was as if he was sitting on a pile of rocks and sticks instead of the smooth bench. He kept lifting one hip and then the other. He squirmed and shifted his feet.

At one point they rode down a steep ramp onto a narrow boulevard beside a canal. It was full of dark water that reflected pieces of light from the windows shining in the buildings on the opposite side. Up ahead, Joe saw two figures standing near the edge of the canal. He was too far away to see exactly what they were doing. When they got closer, he saw a man standing in front a woman whose heels were dangerously close to the edge. One slip and she'd fall in.

Joe was about to shout when he realized the woman wasn't really in trouble. Instead, the man's arms were wrapped around the woman's waist. His head was lowered over her shoulder, and the woman leaned against his body with her head tilted up close to the man's face. It looked as if she was nuzzling his neck or whispering something in his ear. The two seemed oblivious to the wagon's approach. They didn't move or startle or even look while Joe stared at them. That's when he saw the woman wasn't whispering at all, but rather her lips were pressed tightly against the man's lips. They were lovers. Joe looked at Mary to see if she saw them, to see if she also saw the lovers. He figured she hadn't since her hat was pulled so low over her brow.

Further along they turned and crossed over a bridge. It had a small tower in the middle of it with a lone yellow window at the top. They followed the street ahead. The horses' hooves clomped on the stones beneath. The street ended at a crumbling building. The brick walls were mostly knocked away, leaving jagged ridges like broken teeth. They were at the corner of Ludwig and 10th. To their right was an old church.

Joe never really thought about what to expect when he saw the church, but it certainly wasn't what he now witnessed. It didn't look anything like the temple back home, which was a simple one-room building and not like the enormous, spired structure they were getting closer and closer to. Finally they stopped out front. Lamps along the church's parapet spread a ghostly pattern of light and shadow up and down the ornate façade. The effect was not unlike the spooky glow from a lantern playing across someone's face in the dark.

This must be the place, Joe thought. He stepped out onto the deserted street and waited for Mary to scoot across the bench before he helped her down. Then he pulled up the floorboards and dug out the bundle of diesel in the hidden compartment and set it on the ground. He turned to look at the church again, veiled in those strange patterns of shadow and light. He wondered how a person could worship in such a monstrous building.

Joe still didn't like the fact that he had to take Mary with him. He didn't want her to be in any danger, but as Mary said before they left, "We've come too far to stop now."

Joe pulled the deerskins off the container of diesel and tossed them aside. With one hand he grabbed the handle and with the other he clasped Mary's hand. At the wrought iron gate, he stopped for a moment to let his nerves calm down before he pushed open the gate. The hinges screeched in the dark stillness. They both walked up three concrete steps onto a cracked slab inlaid with stones. Up ahead were three large wooden doors. Above each one was a triangle with a dot inside it like a peeled open eye. When they arrived at the middle door, Joe noticed a white button off to the side below a small box perforated with holes. He pressed the button and heard a low buzzing sound.

A few seconds passed and then a staticy voice spoke from the small box. Despite the crackling, there was something familiar about it. It had a measured calm to it that he'd heard before.

"Welcome," the voice said. "Nice to finally meet you. After I buzz you in, proceed to the doorway on your left and ascend the stairs."

Inside was a vast empty hall. Along the sides were statues of bearded men wearing robes and crowns on their heads. At the far end sat three sets of stairs that led up to a bay of dark windows. But that wasn't what caught Joe's attention the most. He was astonished by the huge vaulted rafters made of timber. They spanned the domed ceiling like exposed ribs. He was equally astonished at what was carved into the base of each one—a winged creature with bugged eyes and a long tongue curling out of its open mouth. Hanging from the tip of every other tongue was a long chain ending in a ring of dim lights that dripped spots of light on the floor below.

To the left was a dark archway. Joe figured that must be the doorway the voice referred to. They walked across the huge stone tiles, their steps echoing softly in the hall, until they reached the archway's threshold. In front of them was a winding staircase hollowed into the wall like a cave. Small dots of light were embedded along the edge of each step. Joe slid his foot tentatively onto the first step, as if he wasn't sure it was going to hold him. He didn't get very far before he had to stop. He was holding Mary's hand but she wasn't moving with him. Their arms hung between them like an umbilical cord.

"Come on," Joe said. "Don't be scared. I won't let anything happen to you. Just keep hold of my hand and you'll be okay."

Mary didn't say a word. She merely followed him onto the step. He knew the only reason she did was because of the trust she had in him. She followed on faith, on faith in him.

A little later, they reached the top of the winding stairs where they found another door with a small box and a white button beside it that he pushed.

"Come in, friends. Come in."

A buzz sounded, a latch clicked. Joe picked up the diesel and pushed the door open with his shoulder. Inside, a flood of light smashed into his face. It was in such stark contrast to all the darkness they'd just been in that it momentarily paralyzed him. The room was as brightly lit as noonday on the plains when Joe had to squint to see. He couldn't believe all the light.

"Welcome to my paradise," the voice said. "My island oasis, my tropical wonderland."

Once Joe's eyes adjusted, there was no question it was a wonder to behold. He could hardly believe what he saw. The fear and trepidation that dogged him before had suddenly vanished. The first thought that came to his mind was *beautiful*, although he couldn't articulate a reason for that. It was simply the first impression that came to him. Then he thought of the story about how Virid created the earth as a fertile paradise for humans to live in, a paradise that would last forever as long as people didn't fall prey to their own power. Of course, people did fall prey. That's why the Prophet Roy came. He came to say that Virid spoke to him and she told him she had created a new paradise in heaven for those who trusted and followed in her way. But Joe's next thought was that this couldn't be true, this couldn't possibly exist, and none of it was real.

At the far end of the room, surrounded by palm trees and a waterfall, sat a man in a huge wicker chair. His face was hidden by some kind of ghoulish mask. It looked like it was made of wood. The eyes were painted white and so was the huge snarling mouth. He wore a robe of red fabric with white flowers, which was knotted at one shoulder. Behind him was a huge photo mural. Joe had never seen anything like it in his whole life.

The picture was of a topless young woman with dark brown skin like Ava's. She wore a skirt with the same pattern as the man's robe, red with white flowers, which was tied around her hips. A breeze blew against the fabric and made her long black hair flow behind her. She was looking over her shoulder at a bay of rippling blue water and green mountains that stretched into a big blue sky. Next to the waterfall was a large panel photo mural of another naked young woman. She too had long black hair flowing behind her. Above her head she held some kind of gourd, which dripped clear liquid into her mouth, liquid that spilled down her neck, across her breasts, and over the most arresting part—her round pregnant belly.

The rest of the walls followed the same pattern as the two photo murals. They were covered from floor to ceiling with photographs and paintings of young women, waterfalls, lush forests, sandy beaches, blue waters, and green mountains.

The man eased himself out of his chair and spread his arms wide as if he wanted to embrace them, as if he was their father who'd just returned from a long trip and Joe and Mary were supposed to rush into his arms. Of course, that didn't happen. With the ghoulish mask, he looked more like a demon than a man.

"So you like what I've done to the place," the man said. "Normally, I'd be surrounded by a bevy of GeMs and Amalgams."

"Is this for real?" Joe said.

"It looks like a dream. Like the visions in your sleep before you wake up."

At that moment, Joe recognized the voice behind the mask. He couldn't be sure, but the voice sounded exactly like the voice of the Minister of Peace and Security he saw on television. Despite that revelation, and the web of connections between Ava and Templeton, it was nothing Joe was going to dwell on. He didn't care who it was, just as long as he got the money for the diesel.

"Every man has a dream," the minister continued. "Mind you, this is only but a taste, because this place does exist. Beautiful young women. So much fruit that it lays wasted on the ground because people can't eat it all. The oceans around it teeming with fish. Fresh water cascading from the mountaintops. It's heaven. Only it's not cheap getting there."

"So you haven't been there?"

"Not yet."

"Then how do you know it's real?"

"Look at the evidence all around you. Besides, I know the very man who took these pictures and painted these canvasses. He's back at the islands right now with all the money I gave him for all this."

It must be true, Joe thought. Or at least he wanted it to be true. As he looked around the room again, his eyes settled on something he hadn't noticed at first, a long table with various artifacts on it—statues and carvings and trinkets. There was a magnificently colored stuffed bird with a bright red breast, an orange beak, and a green and purple crown.

"Are those from this land?" Joe said.

"Yes, of course. Come see them. Browse about. Your little companion probably wants to see the young girls with child."

It didn't register in Joe's mind that they were being separated. Mary was going one way, and he was going the other way, which left the minister in the middle, right between them. "The vigilant heart," says the Viridian proverb that Joe knew well, "never wanders." But Joe remained too fascinated and too taken in by the false splendor and the magical promises that all the items in the room offered that he didn't take into account the position he'd put them in. He stood at the table with his back turned, with the diesel still clutched in his hand, and stared at the objects, especially the brightly-colored bird. He couldn't get over the vividness of the colors. And he couldn't get over that such a place as this could be real. Yet here it was. It existed.

The stories were true, then. There *were* "promised lands." No dust. No wind. No cracked dirt. No withering crops. No shortages of water. No hungry nights. A true land of plenty. He'd always been told that the only true "promised land" was Welkenglebe. Any other promises were hollow dreams that led to ruin. He wanted to believe that what he saw in the room was real, especially since the stories of "promised lands" always captivated him. Maybe this was it.

Like the minister said, all the evidence was here. On the table were woodcuts, stone carvings, totems, and clay pots, all illustrating that fact. But there was also something else, an old pistol lying on a snakeskin. The metal was tainted with patches of rust. Joe lifted it off the table. It was heavy in his hand.

"Whose gun is this?"

The minister didn't answer right away. And when he did, his voice sounded rushed and a bit startled. Once again Joe didn't pick up on this sign of trouble.

"Gun? Yes, gun, of course. It was retrieved from a cave on one of the islands. The cave was a pirate hideout. Supposed to belong to a Captain Nero."

After Joe set the pistol down, he heard some rustling behind him, followed by what sounded like a squeak, and then what was definitely a grunt. He stood still a moment. All the clues that he'd missed before began to add up and came rushing into his mind all at once. He dropped the diesel and wheeled around to find the very thing he feared most. Mary's head was caught in the noose of one of the minister's arms. The snarling white mouth in his mask seemed to be laughing now. He held a knife to Mary's throat. Her feet dangled off the floor.

What made it even worse was how Mary's body hung slack and silent, as if accepting that this violence was what she needed to do. It was her sacrifice in order for them to get the money.

"Stop!" Joe shouted.

He charged recklessly at the minister, but then halted abruptly.

"Good choice," the minister said.

He held the blade right under Mary's chin. With one stroke, he could slit her throat.

"Let's be reasonable here," the minister said. "You have something I want, and I have something you want."

"Give her to me," Joe said.

"That's not how it works. This is a matter of negotiation."

"There is no negotiation. Let her go."

"That kind of strategy isn't going to get you far, especially when I have more leverage than you."

"I don't care. Just let her go. You can have the diesel. I don't want any money. Just let her go."

"That's just it. I don't care about the diesel, either. I'm more interested in who sent you. And what kind of operation they have going on. There has been a rash of small-time smuggles recently. I'm beginning to think it's some kind of coordinated effort or a distraction perhaps. When you appeared on the radar screen, I saw my chance to get to the bottom of it. If you give me what I want, your little girl lives. And if you work with me, you get your money." He nodded toward a briefcase beside the wicker chair. "So now that I have your attention, who sent you?"

"No one sent us. I don't know what you're talking about."

"You expect me to believe that two teenage dirt-eaters just happen to come into possession of nearly five gallons of diesel? You are insulting my intelligence."

For a second, Joe thought about making something up that would satisfy the minister, but even if he did, this man seemed like the type that would kill Mary anyway. He must've killed Templeton and Ava, after all, or at least his minions did. At the same time, though, Joe had to find a way to get Mary free and then find a way to get out of there. He couldn't panic. He just had to think.

Then he had an idea. He stuffed his hand in his pocket and felt for the three rifle shells he still had left. He didn't know if they would fit the rusty pistol or not, but he knew the shells were .22 caliber, and many types of guns took that kind of ammunition. Joe glanced to his side. He stood about three steps away from the pistol. But in the time it took him to grab it, load it, and fire it, the minister could have easily killed Mary. However, if he created some kind of diversion that took the minister off guard, he might have enough time. Of course, the question remained if the pistol would even fire.

"If you don't want to cooperate," the minister said, "I can make this even more difficult. Would you rather I torture her right here in front of you? Would you rather hear her scream in pain? I'm making this easy on you, but evidently she doesn't mean that much to you."

Even though Joe was angry at the remark, he didn't lose his temper. He didn't take it personal in the way he would've a week ago when he probably would've flown off the handle and gotten them both killed. In fact, he used the opportunity to slowly pull the shells out of his pocket.

"Don't say that. She means everything to me." He slowly slid both hands behind his back and switched one of the shells to his left hand. "But I'm telling you, I don't know anything. We found that diesel in a wrecked Arbyter."

"What?" the minister said. "That was Operation Dust Storm. They were on a retaliation mission against the SRF. We lost complete contact with one of the units."

"Not anymore!"

Joe raised his arm and whipped the two shells at the minister's masked face. He didn't wait to see if they hit their mark. He lunged for the pistol, snatched it in his hand, and pivoted toward the minister. He swung open the pistol's cylinder. Initially, he couldn't shove the shell in one of the chambers, and he realized they might not be the same caliber after all. His one chance had apparently failed. He glanced at the minister and was surprised to see he hadn't moved at all, as if he wasn't the least bit worried that Joe had a gun.

Then the bullet slid in. Just like that. And he quickly shut the cylinder and pointed the loaded pistol at the minister.

"You're not serious, are you?" the minister said. "That was quite a lot of sound and fury. That rusty old pistol is not going to fire. And if it did, it would more than likely blow up in your face. And I don't want to see you get hurt."

Joe ignored him. He squeezed the trigger. His finger dug into the rusty metal stem. But just like the minister said, the hammer didn't pull, and the pistol didn't fire.

"What did I tell you?" The minister shook his head. "Tell me who sent you and this will all be over. Was it the SRF? Did they threaten your family?"

Joe wouldn't give up. He squeezed even harder. The more he squeezed, the more the pistol shook. It shook to the point where he was afraid if it did fire, he might hit

Mary, so he shifted the barrel further away to the far side of the minister's body. He gripped the pistol with both hands now, with both fingers struggling to squeeze the trigger. It still wouldn't fire. His hands trembled. The pistol shook.

He was about to give up, about to lower the gun, when the trigger finally gave. The hammer snapped back and then slammed forward. The primer cap on the shell ignited. The bullet blasted through the barrel. At first Joe wasn't sure if the bullet had hit anything. He stared at the minister who looked as surprised as Joe that the pistol had fired. The minister pulled his ghoulish mask off and dropped it on the floor. With his face revealed, there was no doubt that he was the Minister of Peace and Security. He looked surprised once again when he turned his head and realized he'd been hit in the shoulder. A trickle of blood fell from the small hole.

"You hit me," he said.

Joe still couldn't believe it worked. But then he panicked, because even though he'd hit the minister, the shot had done little damage. He needed to shoot the minister again. He frantically dug in his pocket for the other shells, only to realize he'd thrown both of them at the minister. They lay scattered on the floor somewhere.

The minister obviously saw what happened. He said, "That's all you got. No more bullets."

Joe had to think fast now. His only plan to rescue Mary had turned out to be futile. He looked at the pistol in his hand and at the long barrel like a stave. It was the only thing he had now. He flipped the pistol upside down. He looked at Mary and then the minister. This was it.

He charged at the minister, not even aware of what he was going to do next. He sprinted across the floor with the pistol held aloft like a dagger. The figure of the minister bounced in his view with each step. Suddenly Joe left his feet. He jumped. He sprang forward as hard as he could. He leapt toward the minister's stunned face. Swinging his arm high, he drove the tip of the pistol right into the minister's eye. He drove it in like a stake.

Even though Joe slammed against the minister's chest, the minister only stumbled back a few steps. Nevertheless, he wailed in pain as Joe fell to the floor. When Joe looked up, the pistol's handle and cylinder were sticking out of the minister's eye, while the barrel was stabbed deep. The minister staggered back some more. He dropped the knife. He threw his hands up into his face, setting Mary free. He grabbed the pistol and yanked it out of his eye. A stream of blood squirted out. Some of it splattered across Joe's cheek and white shirt. The minister's eye was a red gaping hole. He hurled the bloody pistol to the side where it smacked against the photo mural of the pregnant girl before it clattered to the floor. It left a streak of blood across the girl's belly.

Meanwhile, Mary scrambled away and snatched the knife that the minister dropped. Joe got back to his feet. The minister teetered, his hands over his wounded eye. Blood seeped through his fingers and ran down his arms. The pain must've been excruciating because his lips were twisted in a hideous grimace. And then he finally fell to his knees.

Joe threw his arm around Mary and hugged her to his side. She handed him the knife, but Joe didn't see any use for it now. The minister was immobilized enough for them to get away, and there was no sense in wasting time in making their escape. Joe tossed the knife across the floor, but before he turned to leave, he stopped.

He noticed the minister was trying to tap his ear to turn on some device.

"Are you there?" the minister said.

It obviously wasn't working because he kept tapping for a couple more seconds. Then he gave up and started digging in his robe for what Joe figured was his mobicom. The last thing they needed was to have a manhunt after them, so he quickly reached in the minister's robe. The minister tried to grab Joe's wrist, but he was too weak to get much of a grip. Joe fumbled around inside the robe before he found the mobicom. He yanked it out and threw it across the room.

"You'll regret this," the minister said.

Joe didn't pay any attention to him. He turned to Mary. "Let's get out of here."

He took Mary's hand and spun to the door. He meant to grab the diesel before they left, but Mary tugged on his hand and wouldn't move.

"What?" he said. "What is it? Let's go. Come on."

"The money," she said.

She let go of his hand and ran straight toward the minister, who had slumped to a sitting position with his legs sprawled out in front of him.

"Mary!" Joe shouted.

She ignored him. She dashed around the minister's body and squeezed in between him and the chair and grasped the briefcase by the handle. Even in the minister's agony, he recognized what was happening. He tried to paw at Mary to stop her, but he really couldn't see what he was flailing at, and Mary ducked out of his reach with the briefcase.

"Let's go," Joe said.

After he got the diesel, he grabbed her hand again and they ran for the door.

"Stop," the minister shouted. His voice gurgled. "Stop! You can't leave me like this."

Joe turned. The minister's arms lay heavy to his side. His head lolled back and forth. His face was covered in blood, his gaping red eye oozed, and his shoulder still leaked blood.

"Don't just leave me here." Red spittle bubbled at his lips. "Have some decency. Put me out of my misery. Kill me, for God's sake."

"We should help him," Mary said.

"Don't listen to him. It's a trick."

"He's in pain."

"So what? It's not worth it."

He pulled open the door and pulled Mary into the dark winding stairway. They whirled around the steps, ran through the empty hall, and out into the quiet darkness.

When they got to the wagon, Joe lugged the diesel into the hidden compartment. He tried to stuff the briefcase of money in there too, but it didn't fit. He wondered why he was taking the diesel with them, anyway. They had the money, didn't they? It was right there in the briefcase, although he didn't check for sure. He was so used to protecting the diesel, doing everything to make sure it was safe, that it seemed strange to just leave it now. It had served its purpose. There was no sense in trying to smuggle it back out of the city. So he hefted the diesel out of the compartment and onto the street.

He looked at the container for a moment. The reason for their trouble, for their whole harrowing journey, for almost getting them killed, was all for the diesel's money. In that instant, it hardly seemed worth it. All that for a few gallons of liquid that could be burned. That's all. He unscrewed the cap. The burning smell of diesel filled his nose. Then he tipped it over with his foot and watched the fuel darken and glisten the cracked cobblestones.

Chapter 42

The south gate was lit up with lights. It was the quickest way out now. Two turrets sat on the walls on each side of the black gate. Machine gun muzzles stuck out each of the dark windows like spikes on the head of a club. They waited in line as guards scanned people and riffled through their belongings.

There was no one behind them. Mary stirred. She spit on her hand and rubbed it on the dried blood staining Joe's cheek. He noticed the blood splattered across the front of his shirt. He knew the guards would ask about it, so he pulled it off and crammed it beneath the bench. He also tore Ava's bandage off his elbow and tossed it out. He didn't want to give the guards any excuses to question them.

When they reached the checkpoint, the guard that came to Joe's side had pinched eyes that barely opened.

"You ever heard of clothes," he said. "I hope you got pants on in there."

Joe didn't pay any attention. "How far is the nearest town?" he said.

The guard stared at Joe. "I ask the questions around here, not you."

But the guard next to Mary spoke up. "There's nothing until Duncan Ridge," he said. "Four days out."

"It's radioactive," the pinch-eyed guard said.

"That was a long time ago. My second cousin's boyfriend's uncle works for Toxic Reclamation, and the last time they checked they said more people were resettling it."

"Deformed and diseased people."

"Not so much anymore. The defects and stuff have gone down."

Pinch-eyes was annoyed now. "Are you done?" he said. "Because we have a job to do, in case you forgot."

He leaned his head to the side, away from Joe, and looked at Mary. Then he held up his scanner.

"It appears we have a problem," he said.

He leaned his head to the side again to look at Mary.

"What is it?" Joe said.

He was nervous and anxious, not only because of the guards, but also because of the minister. Even though they'd left him terribly wounded, Joe still couldn't shake the sense that he could still find them somehow. Perhaps he had crawled to his mobicom. Perhaps he got the device in his ear to work.

"It says here you came for a breech birth, but it looks to me like that girl still hasn't popped."

"My neighbor Celia had that problem," the other guard said. "Some doctor turned it all the right way, although he wasn't a licensed doctor, on account of him losing it somehow. I think he botched some surgery for an official or something. Anyway, she said he was old, really old, so I guess he knew what he was doing."

"How'd he turn it?" pinch-eyes said.

"I don't know, really. I guess he must've reached inside her and moved it around."

"And then she gave birth, right?"

"No. She went home after that."

Pinch-eyes didn't say anything. He looked at the screen on his scanner again.

"But it says birth on here. So how come she still has the thing if it says birth?"

"I don't know," the other guard said. "Maybe it was a mistake."

"I wasn't talking to you, Darrell."

Joe cleared his throat. He tried to remain calm, but he wanted to push the proceedings along.

"It's just like he said," Joe added. "The doctor turned it around, but she's not ready to give birth yet."

"Where'd you have it done?"

"Public ward."

"Which one?"

Joe didn't know. "Across the bridge," he said.

"Which one?"

"North."

"That's F sector," Darrell said. "I know that one. PW5. My aunt lives around there."

"Would you shut up?"

Pinch-eyes continued questioning Joe. "There's no record on here. If you actually went there, there would be a record. And since there isn't, it means you're lying."

"Wait," Darrell said. "Didn't we get a brief this morning that said there was some transmission glitch in F sector?"

"Didn't I tell you to shut your filthy hole!"

Darrell chuckled nervously and looked off toward the gate. He adjusted his rifle strap.

"Can we go?" Joe said.

"No," pinch-eyes said. "No, you can't."

"Stupid dirt-eater," Darrell said.

"I just wanted to know if you were done," Joe said. "We have a long way to go."

"We're not even close to being done," pinch-eyes said. He looked behind him again. "Get the boys," he said to Darrell. "We're going to conduct a search."

Now Joe wished he hadn't said anything. But that didn't prevent him from wanting to say something more, to tell the guard a search wasn't necessary. He even thought about giving him some money, but then Joe thought the guard might take it all, or accuse him of bribery and arrest them both. As he'd already learned, sometimes pushing the issue only made things worse rather than better. There was nothing he could say or do now that was going to stop the search anyway, so the best thing was to go along with it and get it done quickly.

Joe looked over his shoulder.

"Someone's coming," he said.

Pinch-eyes raised his rifle. "Bring your wagon around to the holding area."

As Joe steered the wagon off to the side of the guardhouse, he saw that the people coming toward the gate were only traders of some sort. They had one large truck box pulled by two bisox and two smaller pickup wagons with campers built in the beds.

Meanwhile, Darrell reemerged from the guardhouse with five other guards following in a line behind him. Pinch-eyes ordered two of them to check the wagons that were rolling to a stop in front of the barrier to the gate. He ordered Joe and Mary to get out of the wagon and made them stand in front of the horses.

"Those are some sorry ass horses you have."

Among the three new guards, one was noticeably taller than the rest. He kept fidgeting like he was uncomfortable.

"Strip down," pinch-eyes said.

Joe was puzzled. He thought they were going to search the wagon.

"You mean take off our clothes?" Joe said.

"Don't get smart with me. Take off your clothes."

"Hey," the tall guard said, "leave them alone." He had a long narrow face that reminded Joe of a garden trowel. He also had eyes that seemed to suffer the feelings of whatever they witnessed. They were the wrong eyes for a guard to have. "They're just simple dirt-eaters," the tall guard said.

"Who yanked your chain?" pinch-eyes said. "I intend to be thorough. I have the authority to conduct any search deemed necessary."

"You know they don't have anything."

"One more word out of you and I'll have you disciplined."

The tall guard glared at pinch-eyes. He gripped his rifle and slid it out from his side and across his stomach in a ready position.

Joe was glad to have someone standing up for them. He hoped it would draw attention away from him and Mary so they could get the search over quicker and get out of the city. Joe glanced at the tall guard to show his gratitude before Joe unfastened the buttons on his pants and let them drop to the ground. After he stepped out of them, he looked at Mary. She hadn't moved.

He leaned toward her. "You have to do it. Then we can go home."

She shook her head, two quick shakes.

"Quit stalling," pinch-eyes said.

Mary flinched, like something jabbed her, and she held her belly.

"For God's sake, leave them alone," the tall guard said again. He stepped forward. "She's pregnant."

Pinch-eyes turned his head slowly to face the tall guard. He looked him up and down. Then he walked casually over to him, only a few steps, but he made them seem longer. He stood in front of the tall guard and pushed up the front of his helmet.

"What makes you so concerned?" pinch-eyes said. "You got dirt-eater blood in you?"

"He's dumb enough, that's for sure," Darrell said.

"No," the tall guard said. "I don't have any dirt-eater in me. It's just common decency. There's no reason to mess with them."

"No reason? Doing our duty is no reason?" Pinch-eyes looked at the other guards before he looked at the tall man again. "I think it's time you learned your duty."

Pinch-eyes gazed up at the dark sky, as if it held a clue to learning duty. Then he swiftly rammed the muzzle of his rifle into the tall guard's groin. The tall guard instantly locked his legs together, hunched over, and pressed his hands to where he'd been hit. But before he crumpled to the ground, he managed to lift his agonized face for a moment and muster a twisted grin.

"Put him in restraints and take him down below."

They trussed him by the wrists and ankles and dragged him away. Joe kept quiet and still. He didn't want to make the wrong move.

When the guards returned, pinch-eyes instructed one of them to help Mary undress. The man stepped quickly up to her, as if he was going to rip her clothes off, but then he stopped and stood still, as if unsure of what to do next. He reached out for her shoulders, but changed his mind and went for her floppy hat. Mary screamed like he was tearing out her hair. She latched onto the hat and tried to wrench it free. Her reaction was the exact opposite of the way she reacted when the minister captured her. Maybe she had had enough. Joe certainly had. He tried to get his hands on the guard to push him away, but two other guards swarmed over Joe and contained him. Darrell grabbed Mary while the other guard grabbed the torn hem of her dress and yanked it up off her body.

"Stop!" Joe shouted. "Stop! Leave her alone!"

"Enough!" pinch-eyes yelled.

The guard stopped, and Darrell let go of Mary. She slumped to her knees. Her yellow hair shrouded her face. Her hat lay crushed and torn on the ground. She shielded her naked breasts with one arm while she cradled her belly with the other. Seeing her like that hurt Joe more than seeing her in the grip of the minister. Or perhaps the emotions were different and that was why it felt worse.

Joe wrenched free from the guards and knelt down beside her. He stared into her eyes. What he saw dug even deeper. Her eyes trembled, but it wasn't out of fear or pain or exhaustion. She looked at him as if he was the only one who ever saw her. He slid his arm gently around her bare shoulders and then slid his other hand across her swollen belly before he helped her to her feet.

Pinch-eyes shook his head at them. "Look at you two pathetic wastes."

"Yeah," another guard said, "that girl looks like she's got a tumor growing out of her."

"Looks like a boil on my ass," Darrell said.

"She don't even look human."

"Worthless dirt-eaters," pinch-eyes said. "We should cleanse the city of dregs like you." He shook his head again. "Get out of here. It's making me sick looking at you."

Joe grabbed Mary's dress and fitted it over her head and pulled it down over her body before he put his own clothes back on. Then he picked up their ratty shoes, and they both got in the cab to finally go.

Chapter 43

The forest road descended along a twisting channel where the air grew colder and damper. Joe dug the bloodstained shirt out from under the bench and put it back on. Dripping moss hung from trees. The darkness grew thicker. Lester and Sam's hooves slipped on the slick, rocky path. The wagon jerked and jounced. They were finally out of the city, but Joe still felt it on his skin, like slimy grease you couldn't wash off.

He kept looking behind him, expecting someone to be there, but all he saw was the black darkness like thick, wet tar. He couldn't get it out of his mind that they weren't still in danger. The deeper they went into the forest, the more he believed that they had miraculously made it out in one piece.

He hadn't checked the briefcase of money yet to see if there was actually money in it. A part of him didn't want to. If there was nothing inside, the disappointment would be overwhelming, especially since they'd dumped the diesel and now they would have no way of getting the money at all. At the same time, he had to know.

He stopped the wagon.

"What is it?" Mary said.

"That case," Joe said.

Joe pulled the floorboards out and yanked the briefcase up onto his lap. He fumbled with the latch until it sprang open. There, on the cloth that lined the inside of the briefcase, sat several fat stacks of bills. He didn't know how much it was, but at least it wasn't empty. Joe should have been happy, but he didn't feel that way right then. He felt relief more than anything. Maybe later, when the events that led up to getting the money receded in his memory, he would feel all the joy he had anticipated from the very beginning.

Besides, their journey wasn't over. But now that they had the money, they could buy needed supplies like food, water, ammunition, and even a new rifle. It was an advantage they didn't have before, and one that could ease their way back home. All they had to do was make it to Duncan Ridge, the town the guards had talked about.

Chapter 44

Near dawn, the dark and dense forest began to lighten. Joe could see the green and brown lichen covering the stones in the road and coating the tree trunks that crowded the roadside. The thick tree branches overhanging their path began to appear against the heap of leaves stirring above. After all the noise of the city, it somehow seemed too quiet, too isolated, too alone.

As the wagon bumped along, Mary convulsed in pain and clutched at her belly more and more. She tried to hide her discomfort by turning away, but it was useless. She groaned and twisted in her seat.

"Is it the baby?" he said.

She nodded and convulsed again.

Believe it or not, he was ready. He wasn't the same boy who left that dusty farm not long ago. For one thing, he totally forgot about the money and everything they'd gone through in the city. He didn't care about being a hero either. It was as if it all didn't exist anymore. It was as if the entire journey had been leading up to this moment instead. He felt a sudden sense of completeness, the kind he thought he would only feel when he finally secured the money. This new feeling swelled inside him. It was like when he stared at a star gleaming in the night and felt strangely connected to it, as though a part of what shined so brightly up there was also a part of him.

Of course, Joe had no way of knowing how their journey would end or how that would change him too. He had no way of knowing what had already happened to his family, that marauders from the north had torched their farm, that the charred bodies of Frank and his mom and his dad were lying in the ashes. He had no way of knowing that after they successfully resupplied at Duncan Ridge, it would take over two weeks to get home, where the happy reunion he imagined would shatter into sorrow, where he would have to dig his family's graves, where he would have to burrow underground to make a bunker and start again.

But all that lay ahead. There was only hope now.

Mary's legs swung open and water splashed on the floorboards like an over-turned bucket. He knew what the broken water meant. He'd seen animals give birth on the farm. A convulsion made Mary double over and rock forward into the dashboard. She was in agony. Joe pulled the reins and the wagon skidded on the slick rocks before coming to a halt.

In the wagon, he made a bed for her by spreading out the dirty blankets. He stripped the shirt from his back to swaddle the baby after it was born. Then he went to her side of the cab. He shoveled his arms beneath her tiny body and scooped her off the bench. He carried her to the back of the wagon where he lifted her higher and cradled her onto the bed. After he crawled in, he knelt beside her and pushed her smashed-up hat off her head. He brushed away the strings of stiff yellow hair crusted to her brow. Her eyes reached out to him like grasping hands.

When he moved in front of her and lifted her torn dress, she immediately snapped her legs shut. He pulled her wet soiled underpants off her thin hips and down her legs. Gently, he slid his hands over her bony knees and pried them open. To his surprise, the crown of the baby's head, shiny and slick, was already pushing its way out. Within a few minutes, it popped through completely. Joe smoothed his hands around the baby's wet head. Bloody liquid spilled over his arms.

A moment later, the child's whole body slipped out, followed by the glug-glug of more liquid. The baby was limp and slippery. The umbilical cord was twisted around its neck. Joe was afraid it wasn't alive anymore. It felt like a stillborn calf, wet and floppy. He quickly unwound the cord from its neck. He grabbed his shirt and wrapped it around the limp baby before he set it on Mary's chest. She cradled it and lifted her head to look at the newborn child. With the back of her fingers, she stroked its tiny cheeks and lips and eyes. She made a soft cooing sound and smiled. The baby still hadn't moved.

"It's ours," she said.

Joe didn't say anything. He thought it was dead. Then all of a sudden the child began to wail.

Acknowledgements

Tremendous thanks goes to the following: my wife, Jessica; my mother, Cynthia; my brother, John; my sister, Amy; my sister-in-law, Verna; my friend, Chris; and my former agent Stephen Barbara, who helped shape this book beyond my expectations.

About the Author

Thomas Christopher grew up in Iowa. He received his MFA from Western Michigan University. His short stories have appeared in *The Louisville Review*, *Hawai'i Pacific Review*, *Redivider*, *The MacGuffin*, and *Valparaiso Fiction Review*. He was also awarded an Irving S. Gilmore Emerging Artist Grant and was a finalist for the Matthew Clark Prize in Fiction. He lives in Wisconsin with his wife and two sons.